The Day it ... Forever

Philip Machanick

Author:	Machanick, Philip, 1957-
Title:	The Day it Rained Forever / Philip Machanick
Edition:	1st ed.
Publisher:	RAMpage Research, 2013.
ISBN-13:	978-1482560992 (pbk.)
ISBN-10:	1482560992 (pbk.)
Subjects:	Climatic changes–Fiction.

Contents

The Day

1   Phone call

THE RAIN pelts down. It rains in summer in Johannesburg, but not usually this much. He picks up the phone, dials the number, more in trepidation than expectation. On the third ring, it picks up. Answering machine.

"When you said, 'see you on the weekend', I kind of expected to find you before the weekend. It's Saturday, 10 am, and I would like to hear from you."

He drops the phone, sags to the floor, no chair handy. Jimmy Anderson, the smartest guy in class, the stupidest guy around girls.

How many times has this happened? When it started, it was so good. Being together felt right, natural. They had such fun. They belonged together. Now this. Catch her on a good day, she is cheerful, expecting fun to happen again, but when it should happen, she doesn't show up.

How can I be such a mug? OK, I am no good with girls, and this all seemed so right, so natural. But that was then. It's obviously over. But why does she keep stringing me along?

Let's face it. I'm a spare. Expendable. She can play the field and always have me hanging around if all else fails.

How stupid am I? A physics and maths graduate, and I can't make sense of this. He's lying on the floor now, crying a small puddle. He grins. *I'm in competition with the rain, but at least the rain won't ruin the parquet. Jeez. Won't it ever stop? It feels like it's going to rain forever.*

He feels a strange sensation in his head, tingling, fireworks going off silently, a brilliant white flash. **Not forever. It stops overnight.**

What? Is this it? Am I finally going loopy? Voices in my head?

If you told anyone else, they would think so.

Who are you?

You. Me, I. Your future self, about 1,000 years from now.

What?

You make two great discoveries, in this order. How to conquer ageing. And then, because we aren't that bright, in another 1,000 years or so, you stumble on a trick with quantum entanglement that lets you communicate in this crude way with your past self.

Oh, right. Now you tell me how to do these things so you can exist.

Nice try. But no, I don't have any memory of this event. By interfering like this, I've created a new timeline.

Schrödinger's cat both lives and doesn't live.

Exactly.

So you know what I'm going through now, do you?

With Mel? Absolutely. It's hard to pick an exact time to push into your event stream. Moments of high stress that can lead to big decisions kind of jump out, times when the

timeline could split.

And this visitation is not in your timeline?

Exactimo. We have bifurcation.

Flashing lights in my head?

You tell me. I've never had someone split my timeline on me. Or if I did, I couldn't tell, or didn't think anything of it at the time because I didn't know what was happening.

So what are you here for? Rescue me from my abject failure to figure out Mel?

Oh, no. You've figured her out all right.

Expendable. Substitute, not clearly for what.

He feels a nod in his head, a weird sensation.

As far as I could tell. I didn't follow her life in detail to the end.

So what is *this about? Not me/us?*

No. Anyway, how would you put this to Mel? She causes you 1,000 years of misery? She'd either think you were crazy or trying to punish her in some sort of weird way. She made her choices, whether they make sense or not, and I couldn't figure them out in a very long lifetime. I need to tell you a bit about my world, how it got that way. There are a few critical points where one individual with foreknowledge can change things.

So save the world?

Yes.

Not me.

No.

Damn.

I knew you'd agree.

Damn inability to lie to myself.

That, my lad, my junior me, is the crux of the problem. You/I/me are unusually honest in that way, if a bit in denial over Mel. Many problems leading to the disaster I now live with start with people willing and able to lie to themselves.

So we are going to save the world for philosophers.

Sorry, we can't keep killing time. Literally. Every second I spend here is a second out of my consciousness back in my own time. It costs me big time in energy and concentration. Just let me give you the scoop, OK?

The scoop? Jimmy feels awe for his older self's enhanced vocabulary and settles in for a monologue.

OK, so this is how it is. Humanity is reduced to a few thousand people, leading a hand-to-mouth existence. I've accumulated what's left of energy sources, people with education and technology. The whole planet's trashed: every major coastal city of your time is deep under water, we have no oil worth speaking of left to drill, natural gas is pretty much gone too, and biodiversity has crashed. I live in a kind of zoo or land ark where I've kept going what I can, but I spend most of my time scrounging for food, and feeding my biogas converter. And I lead the good life for my day.

Think of that: no New York, no Shanghai, no London, no Cape Town. All gone.

How did we get there?

Well, I told you about lying to yourself. It started with the tobacco industry, who decided that the obvious evidence that their product was dangerous, causing cancer and a host of other nasty ways of dying like losing limbs when your circulation falls apart, wouldn't put them out of business if they lied to the public and confused popular opinion about the science.

That's not lying to yourself, that's lying to the unwashed masses.

Getting there. Naturally if the tobacco business said things in their defence, they would run into "they would say that" skepticism. So they set up a front organisation that was supposed to be about opposing junk science, which turned out to be anything bad for tobacco. And populated this entity with retired scientists, who had a thing about government interference in the economy. And that's where the self-deception kicked in. These people actually believed there was something wrong with the science, even though it was way outside their field.

So the world dies of nicotine poisoning?

Nope. That was bad but it didn't stop there. The tobacco people realised it would look a bit suss if they only ever talked about tobacco, so they had their shills talk about other things too, including the ozone hole and global warming.

Now you're losing me. What's a shill? What's the ozone hole? And global warming?

Shill: American for someone who sells enthusiastically. Don't worry about the ozone hole. That's about 5 years off. Global warming also is a way off getting into the media, but that's the big one. Carbon dioxide is a greenhouse gas, it absorbs infrared, slowing the escape of radiation to space, and that warms the planet.

Surely not that many people smoke.

Idiot. This is serious. CO_2 emissions from industry

are growing exponentially. Luckily the temperature effect is only logarithmic, but a linear increase in temperatures is bad news.

Why? If it gets a bit warmer, so what? Anyway, if it got serious, couldn't we stop?

It's a whole lot more complicated than that. Look: the science on this develops pretty well over the next ten years. Just follow it. A few highlights: habitat is highly temperature dependent. Warm the planet and species migrate towards the poles and uphill, pushing those needing lower temperatures off the planet. Ice sheets disappear a lot faster than they form, and are important to regulating climate. So once you lose an ice sheet, you're into not only higher sea level but also warmer temperatures until the next ice age.

Now hold on a minute, are you talking about ice sheets like the Antarctic? Isn't that so massive it would take thousands of years to melt?

So many scientists thought. But it's not that simple. Half of the West Antarctic ice sheet is anchored below sea level, more than 2km below sea level at its lowest point. Destabilise that and it comes away really fast.

Is that what happened?

West Antarctic was one of the bigger ones. A big chunk broke away, about two metres worth of sea level. Anyone close to the area – southernmost part of South America, the Falklands, had an instantaneous rise of many metres before it settled back. We don't know exactly: no witnesses. Every major city in Australia flattened, all the coastal cities around the world pretty much gone, even in the north, where it was

closer to two metres by the time it hit – but that wasn't the end of it.

Another big chunk of ice?

Eventually. But first, isostatic rebound.

Isostatic rebound?

That weight of ice squashes the bedrock down, up to a kilometre in West Antarctic. Release the weight and it rebounds. Do that on this scale with ocean on top, and you get the mother of all tsunamis.

Motherf–?

Not what you're thinking. One Saddam Hussein in a decade or so from now talks about something like the mother of all wars. Anyway whatever was left of coastal cities was completely flattened by this one. Worse than a nuclear war, except no fallout, or so we thought. Then the next big disaster. Methane. There were billions of tonnes of methane in a kind of icy structure called methane hydrates in the oceans. With all this ice gone, the Southern Ocean warmed rapidly. And methane popped up all over the place, causing a rapid spike in warming.

So methane is also a greenhouse gas? As bad as CO_2?

Way worse. It's in low concentration in the atmosphere so it has a much bigger effect if you add some. Though in a few decades it's mostly broken down to CO_2. Short term though it was enough to make a whole lot more ice go.

Wait, wait. Wouldn't the oceans cool with so much ice added?

Yes. But only where the ice was present. The bigger effect was losing ice over a big area of sea, and sea water is much darker than ice.

Ah.   The lower albedo means more of the incoming sunlight is retained as heat.

Now you're thinking. I was beginning to wonder if you did physics this timeline.

So we have a big increase in ocean temperatures at least in selected areas plus massive churning up of the oceans. No one knows which was the trigger, but a massive amount of methane was released, causing a huge spike in warming. That took care of the rest of the West Antarctic, which slid into the ocean much faster than anyone predicted, and the rest of the ice sheets inverted the meaning of the word "glacial" in their pace of sliding into the sea.

With sea level how much higher?

By the end of the century, about 10 metres and rising fast.

By 2000?

No, next century.

Oh, yeah, the thousand years thing. Haven't got my head around thinking that long term yet.

Look, I don't have much more time to keep talking. We have to fix this.

So your life is better?

No, no. I'm stuck with my timeline. I can't change my own past. But I'm pretty sure an informed individual can push the right buttons to change things for the better.

Like tell a few key people to study this stuff up in advance?

No way will that help. Scientists know enough early enough. Remember the lying to yourself thing? That's what we have to counter. Here are a few ideas to start with, I hope you can work with them and think up some of your own.

First, it's a PR game. So get in early, and counter it with even better PR. You'll need a top-rank PR firm, and that takes money. So this is where foreknowledge kicks in: Apple Computer stock slips to about $13 in the late 1990s. The company recovers big time. In about 20 years, if you bought at the minimum, which you know so you can look out for it, your stock would be worth more than 100 times your initial investment.

So if I had money buying Apple stock would be a dead cert? Must admit, they don't look like much right now, though they own the toy computer market. IBM has wiped them out of the business market and increasingly the academic market. Shouldn't I invest in IBM?

Can't be sure of predictions.   Interfering with the timeline could have other effects, and a sudden infusion of capital to Apple could cause them to change vital decisions.

Like?

Bringing back Steve Jobs. Launching into the music and cell phone businesses. Just be careful. But definitely don't invest in IBM. They survive, but they have big downturns.

If I find enough money for this to matter. I suppose I'll find out what a cell phone is by the time this matters.

Right. I'm not going to clutter your head with stuff that will be obvious in due course. Look, that's just one hint. I'll try to get back to you before this all gets too far so I can see how things are going for you with knowledge I didn't have, maybe offer some fresh ideas. You will need to start the PR thing before Apple stock is seriously high, so look out for other ideas. Wait till the Internet gets big.

Internet?

Big worldwide network of networks. Starts to grow out of academia around the early 90s. Anyway, the names to look out for, to invest in early are Google, Amazon, Facebook.

Google,... better write all this down. Apple around 1999, $3, Google. What were the others? Amazing?

I think it's 1997, not 1999. Anyway look for the point where the stock dips below unlucky number $13. Not $3, it doesn't go that low. That's how I remember it. Apple. Amazon, Facebook. If you had money now, which you don't, Intel would be the thing to buy. IBM's PC uses their chip, and they become a near-monopoly, along with Microsoft. Huge compared with where they are now.

But you said Apple... and IBM wasn't the horse to back.

Apple stock goes all over the show. IBM eventually loses their hardware monopoly because their PC design is too easy to reverse engineer. Some people think Apple's lost it completely then they have the biggest comeback of all time. If you have money before Apple collapses, buy Intel and Microsoft.

Oh yeah, and one more thing in the lying to yourself department. The oil industry seriously lies about how much oil is left, and the world economy collapses when supply drops way below demand, just before the big ice crash. So work on pushing alternatives to oil early too.

Jimmy feels overwhelmed by the scale of the disasters but finds himself drawn back to the now.

And Mel?

Marries... someone. Makes it clear I/me/you are not

what she's after with no clear reason for that. She invites
you to the wedding. If you're just the same as me, you'll be
there.

You're not over it are you?

Not in a thousand years. Kid, I don't know how to fix
this one. Let's stick with fixing the planet should we?

Before you go: do I join the CSIR? I've got these
application forms, seems like a lot of bureaucracy. . .

I did. I don't see why not. Not a demanding employer,
you get out of the army after doing basics, and a really
great perk is the exceedingly generous allowance they pay
for overseas travel.

My start to taking over Apple Computer?

Not exactly, but it opens opportunities. Sorry, got to go
soon, this is getting too much, and I still have things to tell
you. Cut the small talk. Just remember: find out about
global warming in about 10 years. James Hansen at NASA
will be the big player. Try to build up cash to interfere in the
PR game big time.

And the no ageing, and time travel things?

Can't explain instantly. Start reading up on biology
so I can explain another time when you have the basics.
A few things: epigenetics – stuff that can be inherited
without changing the DNA. What RNA really is: around
2005 an Australian scientist by the name of Mattick does
some insightful work on how DNA is not purely a machine
that codes for protein, and that opens the floodgates to
discoveries you need. Telomeres: they limit indefinite cell
division, and you need to change that selectively.

Hold up while I write this down. OK, what else?

I figured out the ageing thing after I landed a job in a biology lab, ran into it by mistake when developing software for someone else's research. If you get an opportunity to go to the University of California at Santa Cruz, grab it. That's where it all starts. They do some pioneering work on tools for computational biology. Stay with quantum entangling as a hobby if you like it as much as I did; maybe you'll find a need to talk to a past self some time. You won't need that for this project: watch out for biologists who need help with computer science. UCSC is not the only place, just where I got my big break. And keeping up with physics is good: it's what got my foot in the door at UCSC.

And apartheid? How far into your 1,000 years does this go on?

Don't be an idiot. Something that stupid can't survive. Another example of lying to themselves.   The Soviet Union collapses in a few years, the bad guys in charge here can't play the Bastion Against Communism card any more, and throw in the towel. Nelson Mandela turns out better than the country deserves, everyone else in the ANC disappoints, turns out more like the previous bunch than real revolutionaries. The CSIR survives, even more useless than before, on the myth that the ANC has to preserve institutions rather than throw away necessary skills the way the other African countries did. After a couple of elections the National Party joins the ANC.

They do what*?*

Lose out badly on being the official opposition to the liberal bunch, then go where the money is. Really gotta go.

Jimmy's head clears slowly, the *presence* gone for now.

For how long? Did it really happen? He is still on the floor, his puddle dry. Time to stop crying, whatever really happened. And there it is, his piece of paper, with the strange words on it. Which branch of University of California was it? Does he learn some biology on the quiet? His future self evidently didn't for a while. It's all too much. He drags himself up, finds the phone, hanging by its cord, replaces it on the cradle, then lifts the receiver and dials again. The answering machine again. "Mel... I realise the thing between us is over. It would be great if we can be friends. Feel free to talk any time, if... whatever, you need me for anything, you know where to find me."

He feels sick, forces himself to make some lunch, his passion for cooking dulled. *Is there no part of life Mel isn't involved with? He thinks of the nights she'd get back from the early shift at the restaurant and show him how to make another kind of pasta. Gnocchi is the most fun, but it takes time, it's a social thing, you don't do it by yourself.* He isn't sure what he is eating. The phone rings. It is still raining. He doesn't know what time it is but the feeling of just after lunch time doesn't square with the darkness. The contact with future him has totally screwed his sense of time. He puts on a light and picks up the phone. It's Mel. "Doll, what are you talking about?"

"Every weekend it's the same. Some time in the week, you say, 'see you on the weekend' then on the weekend I can't find you. It's not like we live on different planets."

Mel is forceful, hurt. "I just get carried away sometimes with my friends. I promise, next weekend, I'll put you first. No more nonsense about it's over, OK?"

"I would just like to feel that I'm one of your friends." The piece of paper is staring at him, the word Google looking like eyeballs. It's as if an inanimate object can see he's making a fool of himself.

"You are so much more than just a friend," she insists a little too vehemently.

"Listen, I'm applying for a job at the CSIR. If they take me, I get out of most of the time in the army, but the job is in Pretoria, so I may have to move there."

"You know how I hate Pretoria, but if it's to spend time with you, I'll make the effort. I just hope you can cope with whatever time you have in the army."

"Just have to do basics, then they second us back to CSIR."

He can almost see her smiling cheerfully into the phone. "See you on the weekend then?" As he puts the phone down, he thinks, *Stupid, stupid. She's doing it to me again. Same fake commitment, no specific time. Bet I don't hear from her again. Bet if I try to reach her next weekend, no one answers the phone.*

He needs to clear his head, and takes a walk to Melville, and finds a used book store. He finds a whole section on the rise of the ANC and related events, early independent-owned African newspapers, and short stories and articles by writers for *Drum*, a magazine he vaguely remembers. He buys a selection, and starts reading them in his spare time.

The ANC, it turns out, has a venerable history going back to 1912. Some amazing people pushed the cause of civil and political rights when many white South Africans still resented the end of slavery, or thought the height of tolerance was ending Boer War enmity between English and Afrikaans South Africans.

Jimmy reads with interest about Smuts, the Boer War leader who converted to the British cause, and became a favourite of Winston Churchill. Despite Smuts's role in defeating fascism and the founding of the UN, he could not see past race when dealing with South Africa. Did he not know any of these ANC pioneers? Albert Luthuli, Pixley Ka Izaka Seme, Z.K. Matthews, John Dube, Sol Plaatje, Henry Nxumalo, Todd Matshikiza, Helen Joseph, all great characters who rose above their times. He is especially touched by a short Matshikiza book, *Chocolates for my Wife*, about the tribulations of life under apartheid and in self-imposed exile. The thought of going into the apartheid army makes him feel sick as he reads this. *CSIR. I won't be shooting anyone. Maybe even wasting good government money that could go to killing someone.*

The next weekend, he focuses on getting his application to the CSIR right, and doesn't touch the phone, though it has an indescribable gravitational attraction he can barely resist.

2 Council for Scientific and Industrial Research

T HE CSIR in Lynnwood, Pretoria is an imposing campus. The route there from Johannesburg takes you on
one of the busiest highways in the country, the business
hub of the city metaphorically exchanging bodily fluids with
the political hub on a daily basis. Off the highway, there's a
short section of suburban road, dry and dusty in winter but
resplendent with jacaranda blooms this time of year. Jimmy
drives his car to the gates in some trepidation, worrying that
he was breaching protocol checking the place out ahead of his
interview. At the gate he has to sign in, and notes a number
of people in military uniforms among those signing in. He
checks his watch. *Just as well the meeting is for 11 am. I
wonder how much earlier I would have had to start to make
it through the traffic to get here at 9.*

An officious bureaucrat, pointedly talking Afrikaans
despite Jimmy's obvious preference for English, checks his
ID and produces a map. "Dokter Smit se gebou is hier," she
says, pointing out where Dr Smit's office is to be found, and

highlighting the route on the map to be pointlessly helpful. After all the campus is not *that* big. *I could find it if I walked in from here and checked every building, but I suppose it keeps someone in work.*

"Thank you mevrou," he uses the Afrikaans honorific with deliberation, noting she has a wedding ring, so it's Afrikaans for "Mrs" (or in context, "ma'am"), to show he is not incapable. Or *tweetalig* – "bilingual" – as anyone fluent in Afrikaans is called in the public service. She stares at him through stern glasses all the way back to his car, registering no awareness of his pedantic musings.

Dr Smit's office is in an anonymous building of brick and glass. Jimmy arrives at the office door a minute or two early, and loiters, waiting for the second hand to cross 12 before knocking. He has a slightly tatty bag in one hand, and holds it nervously, worrying if he should have bought or borrowed something that looked more professional. He hears a muffled sound from within, then the door opens.

"Ah, you must be Mr Anderson, the student who wants to work here." He offers his hand. As Jimmy shakes it, the doctor adds: "Very perspicacious of you to call around ahead of the interview. The interview is very formal. You can't really get the measure of the man from that, and you need to know if you can work with us too." His diction is extremely precise, that of someone speaking a second language and wanting to show off his prowess.

He ushers Jimmy into the office. "Sit, sit."

Jimmy sinks slightly into a chair that isn't generously upholstered, with hard wooden arms. "Well, my lad, I believe you are planning on going into the army in July."

"Dr Smit, you don't really plan that. I asked for exemption because my honours programme goes on to January, and they deferred me to July."

"Be that as it may young man, that gives us a good start. Should you be appointed, you will have the best part of half a year to become acquainted with the organisation, and can fit right in again should you be so lucky as to be seconded back here."

At Jimmy's surprise, he laughs. "Don't worry, if you get the job, you will be here right after basics. Once you've learnt to march and use a rifle, you can get right back to doing science. Unfortunately we can't pay you your full salary while you are in the army, but I do know a few tricks to help you with the income. But enough about that. Let's talk science."

Jimmy nods. "Doctor, I am curious to understand what attracts you here rather than to a university."

"Ah, good question. CSIR was set up in 1945 to be the country's premier science body. We only do science, no teaching. We don't have the publish or perish pressures, so we can sit back and think about the bigger questions. Nowadays, it's not quite that idealistic. People in government are starting to talk about making everything pay its way. But still, I like it here: not as many distractions."

"Doctor, I brought you a copy of my honours thesis. Could I leave it with you?" He produces it from the bag. "It's a survey of the quantum theory of magnetism. I don't know if CSIR is doing anything that theoretical but I think it demonstrates that I can pull together a range of sources into a whole."

"Thank you, this looks interesting. It's been a while since I read something like this. You are right, we are a bit more applied here, but it's good to see you can write." Dr Smit puts the bound volume down carefully on his side of the desk, and smiles. "I'll make an effort to read it before the interview.

"Now, would you like to meet some of the others in the department?"

They walk around, Dr Smit knocking on doors and introducing people. After a while, he says: "Why not stay for lunch? You can meet people better that way. I have a little work to do before then, but you can read some of our technical reports while you wait."

"That would be great, thank you very much."

Dr Smit ushers him to a reading room lined with shelves of reports. The titles all look very applied, and he wonders if any of this is published. "Thanks, doctor, this should keep me busy." He smiles politely and Dr Smit leaves him to it. He pulls down a thickish report describing a new programming language, with no obvious point to it. *I did computer science for only two years, so maybe I'm missing something, but shouldn't this thing explain why they want a new language up front?* He's still staring at it when he becomes aware with a start of a physical presence.

"Sorry, did I take you by surprise? Name's Nooby. Not my real name, everyone calls me that."

"Nooby?"

"Kind of a joke thing. I showed up at a student club when I was young and fresh, and started asking lots of questions. One of the old hands said, 'Listen to the newbie go,' and it kind of became my name. Anyway, why are you reading about that useless programming language? Smit told me you were into theoretical physics."

"Oh, this? I just picked up the first thick report I found."

"Thick is right."

"You're being rather rude about the nation's premier science body."

"Ah, you had the spiel too. It's nothing like that. Sheltered employment for incompetents."

"And you?" Jimmy suddenly takes in the army uniform, the hair that somehow fails to look regulation despite being cut short, the cynical gaze. "A low-maintenance draft dodger?"

Nooby laughs. Discretely. "Not so loud. They take this stuff seriously here. They tolerate me because I have a clue about how to write a decent paper. Helps them if I put their name on, helps me. Better than marching around a parade ground or being shot at out in the sticks."

"Well, I do have some illusions that I can do good science here and definitely no illusions that I can do good science on a parade ground or being shot at."

"Yeah, well, just make sure you fit in and don't get in too much trouble, and you'll do fine. It's only two years after all, after the truly intolerable time you have in basics. And besides the crap shovellers, there actually are some good people here."

"You got through basics."

"And you think I don't look too physical? It was pretty tough on me, I can tell you. When are you shipping out?"

"July intake. Upington."

"Holy crap. Have you any idea what Upington is like

in winter? There's only one thing worse than Upington in summer when I was there and that's Upington in winter. Tell you what. While you wait for Smittie, I'll give you some survival hints."

"Please. Can we go outside? Talk of terrible cold makes me hanker for the summer air."

The grounds turn out to be pleasant enough for walking around. "OK," Nooby starts, "you need to take a good bunch of kit in with you to start. You can buy stuff there but shopping time is limited, and it's cruelly expensive. Have you got something to write with?"

Jimmy rummages in his tatty bag and pulls out a pad and pen.

"Great, so first you need a good length of chain, a metre or two, to tie your stuff together. Half a dozen small padlocks. Brown shoe polish, Kiwi brand. Shoe brush. Lots of elastoplast. You will get blisters from hell the first time you do a route march. Small towel. They give you towels but you need them pristine for inspections. Good collection of twenty cent coins for the phones. Aerogrammes to write begging letters home without having to keep track of stamps. Pens to write the begging letters."

"Is that *all*?"

"No way. There's a ton of stuff I've forgotten. Maybe we can meet up on a weekend. Meanwhile you need to extend your vocabulary. There's an Afrikaans word for everything in the army. In fact, there's *only* an Afrikaans word for everything in the army. Your metal trunk you store stuff in is your *trommel*. Your duffle bag is your *balsak*."

"So much for two official languages."

"Well, quite. We are still fighting the Boer War but the poor Blacks keep getting in the way. But you aren't here to talk about that. Tell me about your theoretical physics stuff."

"Yeah, well, I think there's lots interesting yet to be discovered in quantum physics. For my honours project I did a survey of the quantum theory of magnetism, but that's just a start."

"What sparked your interested in quantum theory?"

Jimmy stops to shift his gaze up a tree. This somewhat intimidating intellect could just be the type to scoff at imaginary friends. "Can't say really, it just kind of grew on me."

"Hah! Brilliant! An impractical mind. We should get on just fine. I should give you a copy of my thesis to read. See what you make of it."

"Thesis?"

"You know, the thing they make you do so you can put doctor in front of your name. Works great for getting off speeding fines."

"Oh, doctor..." Jimmy feels a bit weak. He is not used to associating with PhDs; his professors all have intimidating manners, especially the ones whose subjects he cares about in the Physics Department.

"Now, don't go all formal on me. Save it for Smittie. They for sure did not give me much respect at Upington. Anyway. Lunch time. Let's get back."

3   Nooby's World

S ATURDAY.   The trip to the CSIR may have gone reasonably but visiting Nooby is something else. Nooby is a physics PhD, casual attitude masking intimidating put-downs, but hey, you have to start somewhere if you're about to save the world, and Nooby could be the right sort of friend. Jimmy finds parking at the back of a row of shops, with small flats above. Unlike in the CSIR parking lot, his tattered Fiat fits right in.

On the way in he sees a funny sign, **Rent A gent**. *What's that? Are they male escorts?* But the detail is clear, they administer rentals and are too cheap to fix their sign if they ever noticed it contained an extra space. The building is dark brick at the bottom, with pale beige plaster covering upper levels. Nooby is in number thirty-four. Jimmy finds his way up an external flight of stairs and stops when he finds the number. The door is dark wood, perhaps stained; it's almost black, with a couple of thin vertical corrugated glass strips. He is about to knock, then spots a doorbell. His hand hesitates between the options.

What the hell. I'll go high tech. He pushes the doorbell

24

and it makes a rasping noise. A little later, the door opens to reveal a glowering stranger. "Hi, I'm Lukas. Nooby is in the bathroom."

Jimmy decides he's had an invitation to enter so he finds his way inside, the interior cool and dark, with vaguely shaped furniture and piles of papers and books. There is a large room leading to a partially separated kitchen, with two doors off to the side; the one at the kitchen end he guesses must be the bathroom.

A tired-looking girl with tied-back blonde hair emerges from the nearer doorway and pushes past, barely muttering a word as she leaves. Jimmy stares after her, but the door closes with no further communication.

Lukas is very quiet. Jimmy awkwardly sinks into an unevenly padded chair and hunts for something to read. The toilet flushes from roughly the right direction and Nooby is in the room, bouncy as Jimmy remembers him from the CSIR trip. "Hey, Lukas, Jimmo, I see you are getting acquainted." To the ensuing silence he adds, "Lukas was doing undergrad while I was tutoring and we both somehow landed in the same platoon in the army, and then in the CSIR. Lukas is a bit weird but OK when you get to know him. He tolerates me and my irregular social life and I don't ask him about his."

Jimmy looks around and doesn't spot anything more interesting than on his first impression. "I thought the army was, like, being in jail, you know, you have to live in a barracks until they let you out."

Nooby grins. "Normally yes but sometimes you get let out for good conduct or, in our case, the excuse that the CSIR isn't close to a base and we would waste a lot of valuable time commuting. And we can't afford a car on army pay. Oh yes, and we both told them we had an invalid aunt who needed us to care for her. For economy we both used the same invented name." Jimmy looks at the two in turn, trying to work out how much of this to believe. "In any case," Nooby goes on, "Lukas is planning on moving on in July, so I may have a vacant spot here. You could pull the same trick. Rent is not too high and we just about come out on army pay."

Jimmy contemplates. "I'm not sure if I have any aunts with the same name as yours. Or as young as the one who pushed past on my way in."

Lukas grimaces. "Just as well I'm moving out. I'm not sure I could stand two with this sort of humour. But welcome to chez loonybin. Nooby will teach you how to cope with the emotional sterility of the military life with a succession of empty relationships." He stares at Jimmy, who keeps emotion in check. "Tell you what, let's drink to that. Unless you'd like something stronger."

"Now, Lukas, don't frighten the boy off. He's young and impressionable." Nooby points at Lukas's nose and Lukas feigns a sulk, which is pretty much where things started. "Jimmo, tell Lukas what you're after."

"Well, really, just a few hints on how to cope with the army. I hear bad stories about what it's like, but not much practical advice."

Lukas wakes up again. "No girlfriends to blow you away while you're defenceless and emotionally vulnerable, with only a pimply korporaal to look to for affection?"

Jimmy is quietly controlled, but gives away more than he intends. "No."

Lukas grimaces. "Then you needn't take lessons from lover-boy here on how to fill the void with empty sex. OK, boy, I hear you're good at maths."

"Uh, well." Jimmy looks at Nooby.

"Play along, kid."

"Well, yes. I do have a little mathematical skill."

"Good," sneers Lukas, "then get down and give me 100."

"What?"

Nooby points to the floor. "That means 100 pushups. And do it now, no arguing."

Jimmy, in the spirit of the game, jumps out of the chair and does five pushups reasonably easily, but is struggling by the tenth. "Can someone really do 100 pushups?" he gasps, collapsing on his face.

Nooby laughs. "Now you're getting it. If they knew you could actually do 100 pushups they'd ask you to do 200."

Jimmy sits up on the floor. "So maybe I should work on the pushups a bit but make sure it doesn't show?"

Lukas chuckles, his first sign of humour. "You see how it is kid. They try to break you so no matter how ready you are, they push you further. Unless you know the system, and make them think you've hit your limits way before you really have."

Jimmy tries a few more pushups and gives up, collapsing in a heap. "OK," he says as he sits up, "I should definitely practice a few more of those. Anything else?"

Nooby contemplates. "Have you done much running in army boots? No? Find something like hiking boots and run in them. You need to build up some callus, otherwise you get nasty blisters." He looks over to Lukas.

Lukas eyes Jimmy out. "You know the advantages in being Jewish? All kinds of extra holidays, better food, never work on a Saturday."

"I didn't know Lukas was a Jewish name."

Nooby laughs out loud. "Nor is Van der Veen. What did you tell them, Lukas?"

"I told them it was from my mother's side. You are Jewish if you mother is Jewish."

"Is she?"

Nooby hasn't quite done laughing. "As Afrikaans as they come. Melktert and koeksisters."

"But didn't they quiz you on observance?"

"Nah. I told them I wasn't very observant but the State President would hear from my parents if they made me work on the Sabbath. Just as well they didn't check – but mention PW Botha to any of the military and they kak themselves."

Jimmy finally has the energy to get up off the floor. "So Lukas, why exactly are you moving out?"

"I got this buddy who's finishing off on the border in July, and he wants a roommate. Known him forever, the only guy who gets me. Nooby and I creep each other out too much living in the same place."

"Yeah, Lukas and I don't exactly finish each other's sentences. Though we kind of get on when we have to."

Lukas fixes Jimmy with a discomforting gaze. "Anything else you want to know?"

"Uh, no." He spots a book on the couch and points at a familiar-looking name on the cover, Can Themba. "Well maybe. Is this also essential reading in the army?"

Nooby snatches it. "The army would call this subversive.

And much of the CSIR would too. Idiots. They are fighting something they don't understand."

Jimmy grins. "I won't tell if you promise not to tell." He divulges his new spare-time reading habit.

On the trip back to Johannesburg, Jimmy suddenly realises he hasn't thought of Mel all day. *But I'm thinking of her now. How can you unthink something? Was future self really right, that his feeling for her leads nowhere, nohow?*

Getting home trying to unthink becomes all-consuming to the extent that he doesn't know how he did it, navigating as he is from an unfamiliar part of Pretoria.

He gets home and collapses on his bed.

The room spins and he opens his eyes. He isn't sure if it has stopped as he opens his eyes, or if he has re-anchored to reality. Each time he closes his eyes, the sensation restarts. *How can I escape this? Future self, does this go on for a thousand years?*

He feels a strangely familiar sensation in his head, tingling, fireworks going off silently, a brilliant white flash. **Not entirely. But with foreknowledge you can do better. Dammit, getting professional help for this sort of thing is not such a big deal.**

And tell them about the mystery voice in my head, the future me who shows up conveniently at the critical moment? What made you show up now anyway?

I remember this as a difficult time. The initial meeting with Nooby, getting home in a puddle of self pity. I couldn't be sure it would be the same this time around, but I did sense a crisis. Tell me about Nooby. He was a key influence, but I don't remember much, especially early days.

Jimmy summarises and ends by asking: *What of Lukas?*
He seems sharp but flakey.

A long pause.

Lukas? Lukas... doesn't signify.

Doesn't "signify"? What the hell does that mean?

**How old are you now? Twenty-two. How much can you
remember of events of the last decade? That's half your
life. If I met Lukas once or twice a thousand years ago,
why would I know who he was now? I can't remember
everything. Just too much detail. Nooby stuck because
he motivated me to look at some interesting physics, but I
barely remember him. Lukas had no major influence on
future events. Doesn't signify.**

So I should expect Lukas to disappear from the scene?

**My intervention has obviously changed the timeline as
you experience it. Nothing like that is guaranteed. But
please try not to run your life according to what I say, except
where we have an agreed project, like climate change.**

Ah, so we've agreed to that now, have we?

**As I know myself, I would have taken it on. I did, but
too late. Are you in or not? The energy to connect is hard
to sustain. Help me out here.**

Of course I'm in.

Good lad.

*I just wish I could unthink when I get stuck on thinking
about Mel.*

**Get therapy. And anyway you are more attractive to
females than you think. Just don't know how to decode
the signals. Reminds me. The mile high club is not all it's
reputed to be.**

The what?

Sex on a plane. At some point in the future, if your timeline doesn't diverge too much, on a long international flight, a hot number with a stock of duty free Chivas Regal plies you with it to reduce your resistance –

What's that? A kind of scotch? I don't even like scotch.

You'll like Chivas, believe me – and the pair of you end trying the limited angles in a toilet. Too little space to get good angles for anything, and you keep worrying if the fixtures will stand the leverage.

Do they?

Of course. They have to design for obese Americans.

You remembered that well enough.

True. Just something to think about to get you out of a Mel funk.

And no hint of when?

The future presence has gone, this time with an almost audible pop in his head.

So does Nooby *signify? And should I talk to Lukas again, to see if he can add something?*

He grins.

Mile high club. Probably never happens. He visualises the shape and size of an airline toilet cubicle. *And how would two people get in unnoticed, and do anything interesting without being heard? Naah. No way. Probably spent 1,000 years thinking that one up just to lighten my mood.*

The room has stopped spinning. He falls asleep.

4 Basics

B
ASICS TURNS OUT to be all it's promised and more. Korporaals, themselves mostly fresh conscripts from a batch or two back, bitter about how roughly they were treated in basics and their leadership course, are playing the school bully freshly graduated from being bullied. Sergeants, PFs working out their frustrations at not being good enough for a more lucrative career choice – such as making officer, or getting a real job – bark orders, demand impossible physical feats as punishments for trivial infractions and generally make life a misery for conscripts, when the korporaals aren't being sadistic enough.

As promised, everything has an Afrikaans name, and everything *only* has an Afrikaans name. *Trommel, balsak,* and numerous curses that may or may not have an English equivalent.

And the people you share with: for an anti-communist army the South African military is remarkably egalitarian. Jimmy shares his barracks with a weird assortment of people. There's Cloete, who insists on pronouncing his name the German way, and is surprised to be called Clitoris. But Cloete is surprised by everything: he has the intellect of an ostrich, which is to say to a good approximation, none. Jimmy recalls reading somewhere that an ostrich has a brain the size of its eyeball, and Cloete has small eyes. Johansen keeps to himself except close to bed time when he hauls out his smokes and smokes the barracks to sleep. Jimmy tries arguing with him the first time this happens, and learns even more curse words. Kobus is big and silent, and does everything military with effortless competence. He learns to strip down and assemble his rifle blindfold when the rest are still getting it wrong with both eyes open. He marches perfectly, learns every drill instantly and always looks as if his clothes were made on him by the factory.

Then there's communicating with the outside world, the impossible task of finding time to write letters, to make phone calls – the endless hunt for enough 20c coins to phone long distance, and everything is long distance from Upington. From having drifted away from all family connections, he rediscovers the merits of having a mother. It's bitingly cold as he feeds the coins in but her voice instantly warms him a degree or two. Not enough to fool a mother. "You sound as if you're shivering, dear. Should I send you a jersey?"

"No ma. You can't wear your own stuff here and anyway good things don't survive the rough treatment they get here."

"Are they feeding you well enough?"

"The food isn't great but I'm not here for gourmet cuisine."

"Didn't that girlfriend of yours go in for good cooking?"

"Ma, Mel is history."

"Sorry Jimmy. I didn't know you had taken it so hard.

Find youself another nice girl when you get out of there. You don't know what a catch you are."

Not so easy, he thinks. "Ma, the coins are running low. Is everyone OK at home?"

"Your dad as always is tied up in his work, so I'm pretty much alone at home, but we are all getting on pretty well. Are you sure I shouldn't send you a jersey? Some nice food?"

"Ma, some crunchies would be nice even if I have to share them around."

A week later, a package arrives for him, and he makes a few friends by sharing – even if he ends up with only one crunchie himself.

One of the most impossible tasks is making a mil-spec bed – at least for Jimmy. With all the polishing, cleaning and general time-wasting, a trivial task like making a bed elevates to almost unattainable – especially as your korporaal demands an impossible level of perfection, as if your bed is made of a solid piece of wood, cut, planed and sanded to perfect corners. Everyone irons their beds to make them look as good as possible, even though this is strictly contrary to regs.

Their korporaal, one Riggs, apparently trying to out-do his Afrikaans-named colleagues, takes it as a vicious personal attack if he finds any imperfection.

Jimmy can solve a partial differential equation, but he cannot get close to making his bed look mil-spec. Each time the korporaal inspects his bed, he is more infuriated, the bed a personal insult. He flings it to the floor, bedding, mattress and frame going different directions, demanding that Jimmy redo it. In the second week, he returns after fifteen minutes, and pulls out Jimmy and three others chosen at random for collective punishment.

The entire platoon assembles on the dark muddy parade ground in a light but miserable drizzle to watch Jimmy's humiliation, along with the innocent three, who can safely be expected to extend Jimmy's punishment if bullying theory holds – with no personal risk to the korporaal if they go too far.

As the korporaal starts yelling at them, Sergeant Roodt appears on the scene. "What the vok is going on here?" he yells at the korporaal.

"This Anderson thinks he's too good to make his own bed, sersant. He's a vokken science graduate, thinks he's too good for army life," the korporaal barks back.

"And the others?"

"Didn't pull him into line, sersant."

The sergeant rounds on Jimmy. "So Anderson, you think you're clever, hey?"

"*Sersant*, I don't think you have to be very clever to be better at making a bed than I am."

"Ja, well so you are a vokken graduate hey?"

"Er, yes, sersant, but not in bed-making."

The platoon stops laughing very abruptly when the sergeant turns on them, a savage look on his face. He turns back to Jimmy. "A comedian eh? At least you are good at one thing. What else? Ja well, are you good at maths hey?"

Knowing exactly where this is leading, Jimmy nods slowly, and says, "Maybe a bit better than making beds."

"Well then, get down and give me a hundred."

The sergeant stalks off, throwing a remark back at the korporaal, "Riggs, you know what to do, hey?"

Jimmy does a very passable impression of an unfit person battling to do more than 10 pushups, and collapses after getting as far as 20, only remembering he's going to have to wash all the mud off and look presentable by 4am reveille as it hits him in the face.

The korporaal mercifully doesn't inflict any further punishments on the parade ground, and hustles them back to the barracks. Once they are all dutifully standing at attention at their beds, he yells, "Obstacle course!" This turns out to mean alternating going over and under each bed, the barracks ending up in a total mess, trommels emptied out and generally a scene of chaos.

"All right, you vokken scum! Get this place clean for inspection at reveille." The korporaal stalks out, his day ruined. Apparently.

There's a surly silence. Then Kobus speaks up, "Listen, okes, I can make a blerrie bed with my eyes closed. I'll make this idiot's bed if he promises he'll never try to do it himself again." A raucous cheer breaks out, and Jimmy is torn between abject humiliation and gratitude.

His new friend explains himself as he makes Jimmy's bed, disposing of the task in a crazily short time. "Listen, oke, I'm not your vokken servant I just blerrie want to get some sleep. Make sure I'm your buddy. Kobus looks after his buddies. Just don't take advantage." Kobus doesn't look like someone you would cross. He would probably be invited to do 200 pushups if he ever transgressed, but then again, maybe a bullying korporaal wouldn't dare.

"No, no. Listen, I may be useless at some things, but I never let a friend down." He offers Kobus his hand, Kobus shakes it perfunctorily and gets back to the task.

"OK, Jimmy, do my share of floor cleaning then we're square, OK? But I'll blerrie check on it before that asshole korporaal sees it."

Jimmy grins, and gets to it.

Another day, another round of pointless activity. The army's motto: hurry up and wait. Rush somewhere, and find the planned activity isn't ready. Offend the korporaal and run around the parade ground. A march to the rifle range turns to hell when the korporaal decides it would be fun to see how long he can make the troopies hold their rifles above their heads. Jimmy surprisingly is one of the longest hold-outs, forgetting the plan of seeming weaker than he really is. The korporaal doesn't notice, he notes with relief when dropping his arms.

Back in the barracks that night, it turns out that someone else *has* noticed. Johansen for once is in a talkative mood. "Look at health nut here who won't let an oke smoke in peace. Falls on his face doing 10 pushups but he held up a rifle vokken almost as long as Kobus. Bet you *can* vokken do 100 pushups."

Jimmy contemplates. "If I can do 100 pushups will you stop smoking out the barracks?"

Everyone is listening now. Jimmy looks at Kobus. Kobus looks at Johansen. Johansen looks at his boots. "You're on," he mutters.

Jimmy rips off his boots and socks, and gets down. Kobus starts to count, and by the time he gets to 20, the entire barracks is counting along, and no one notices the korporaal walking in. Suddenly Jimmy finds he is in total silence and looks up to see the korporaal's livid face, and collapses, but too late – his secret is out.

"Jou vokken donder! Did you think you would get away with that? Let me see you all do 200, and get down now."

A ripple runs through the troopies, all except Jimmy standing at attention, as they should when an instructor walks in. Something in him snaps, and before he knows what's happening, he is standing up and his fist is ploughing into the korporaal's gut. Riggs suddenly looks small and pathetic – but before this can develop further the pandemonium of the last few minutes has the inevitable consequence: the sergeant walks in and starts yelling at everyone, until he spots Riggs doubled up in front of Jimmy, who is still not standing at attention.

"Riggs! What the vok is going on here?"

Riggs manages to straighten up. "This vokken windgat smartass blerrie assaulted me."

"Anderson! Stand to attention. What the vok do you think you are doing? You aren't in your blerrie university now where you fuck up anyone you like. Assaulting your superiors is big trouble. Insubordination, assault."

Jimmy is feeling faint as he tries to stay as vertical as he can, vaguely wondering how deep the shit has to be to get sworn at in English. But then the sergeant snaps to attention and salutes. A stiff figure with two star shapes on his shoulder, one looking like Cape Town castle, strides in. *Cripes. I've never seen one of those before. How much worse does this get?*

"Sergeant, I heard this commotion all the way from the officers' mess. Explain." He speaks quietly and smoothly, with a chilling precision to his words.

"Kommandant, this troopie assaulted his korporaal."

"I see. Very serious. Trooper, do you have anything to say for yourself?"

Jimmy thinks very fast. "Sir, I was trying to persuade one of the others to give up smoking by showing him that even a weak science graduate like me can do 100 pushups if you don't smoke."

"A science graduate, eh? That should make you clever. You won't feel so clever if you go through the military justice system. How does this all justify assaulting your korporaal?"

"Sir, I'm sorry. I've never done something like that before." He was close to tears but somehow managed to keep control.

The kommandant nods, signs of weighing up options exercising his face. "Sergeant, send this man to my office at 07:00, will you? I will see if I can find a suitable punishment for him that will save the bother of a trial."

Once they are left to their own devices, Kobus pulls him aside. "Listen, oke, you don't know how often I wanted to give that little shit a klap. I can make your bed but you blerrie well stay out of trouble. If the kommandant didn't walk in you would have been on a charge for sure, and you blerrie well better use that stupid clever brain of yours to think of something to say tomorrow to get out of this."

Next morning at 07:00, he's outside the kommandant's office. The officer calls him in, and shoos his aide out.

"Anderson, it looked to me when I walked in there was

more to it than a punch up. What happened?"

Jimmy explains, carefully omitting anything that might incriminate anyone else, but this time giving the real story about smoking.

"Well, smoking in bed is against regs, but how can you police that? If you rat on your buddies you can't trust them when you are in a shoot out on the border. And anyway you hit the bloody korporaal."

"Kommandant, the korporaal keeps picking on me because I'm not the best at things like making beds, and punishing the others for my shortcomings."

"Making a bed is part of the discipline of a soldier. So is not assaulting your superiors. We have to uphold the law."

"But he insists we iron the beds. Isn't that also illegal?"

"Maybe so, but can you prove it?"

"Kommandant, I am really trying but I just can't take it when the others are punished because I'm never going to be a good soldier, and it's pointless anyway to try to make me a good soldier because I'm going back to the CSIR after basics."

"OK, now you may be a graduate but you are a bloody fool. The korporaal will be looking for ways to get back at you if I don't throw the book at you, and in an army camp, that can be pretty dangerous. The CSIR would complain to the bloody president himself if you got killed here but I can't let discipline go. Assaulting an instructor is pretty serious, so we have to do something that looks like real punishment."

He contemplates for a minute. "Anderson, what else are you good at?"

"You mean sir like am I good at maths, which means I do

100 pushups?"

"No boy. If I played that sort of game I would still be shouting on a parade ground. Help me here. We can't punish you by making you do science. What else *can* you do without cocking up?"

"Well, I do like cooking."

"Go on."

"I used to have a girlfriend who worked nights in a good Italian restaurant, and she passed on a lot of tips. We couldn't afford to eat out so we did our own fancy cooking. I like to think I got pretty good." *She certainly didn't walk out on me over* that.

Another Mel moment. But the Kommandant is addressing him, bringing him back to the here and now. "Now you're talking. For some serious punishment you will report to the officers' mess and make all my meals for me. You'd better bloody be good, otherwise no second chances. More trouble with your korporaal and he handles it." He scribbles on a piece of paper. "Take this to the korporaal, and he will take it from there. Are you any good at acting?"

"Maybe a little."

"Make bloody sure you look really upset about your punishment."

"Yes sir."

The officers' mess is pretty big. Upington is after all a major training camp. Jimmy goes there on his own, not sure what to expect. He finds a back entrance, and asks to speak to the person in charge, and is told, "That would be Sergeant Truter." He is led through the kitchen to a large chef, muscular in a fat kind of way, with sergeant's stripes on his shoulder.

He starts to speak but the sergeant interrupts. "Ja, so you're the gourmet chef. This is a busy kitchen. You can do the hell what you like but don't get in the way." And see how long you last, his body language says.

"Sergeant, just one question. Where and when does the kommandant take his meals?"

"Get his breakfast ready by 06:00, lunch by 13:00, dinner by 18:00 and someone will be here to fetch it. Try to work off supplies already out for the others. I don't want to go to stores just for you. Now bugger off and get on with it."

Jimmy consults his watch. He has fifteen minutes to make lunch. He looks around, identifies where various supplies are to be found, and gets to it. *What can I do in 15 minutes? A nice carbonara.* He is looking for spaghetti then decides to go for the bold approach: hand-made pasta. It ideally should be rested before cooking, but he's cooked it before straight from rolling and cutting. He incorporates eggs into flour, working more by feel than recipe, kneads the dough energetically to get it smooth, and rolls it very thin, leaving it on a floured board, while working eggs up into the sauce, and boiling up some water. That done, he cuts the dough into thin strips, gives them a twist and tosses them in the boiling water. He drains them, and is tossing them on the sauce as he hears over his left shoulder, "Where's the kommandant's blerrie lunch?"

"Right here." He grabs some of the grated cheese going into whatever the other officers are getting, tosses it on, not parmesan, but you have to make do – and finds some chopped parsley, which he adds for colour.

That night the sergeant joins the korporaal for inspection. For once the beds are good enough. The sergeant dismisses the korporaal, a break from convention, and pulls Jimmy aside. "I don't know how you blerrie did it but the kommandant himself asks me to keep you out of trouble. And keep up the punishment duties until you're out of here." He winks, and leaves Jimmy to contemplating how this all could have happened – and inevitably starts thinking of Mel again, how she showed him how to make a perfect carbonara without scrambling the eggs...but his time is not his own. Kobus grabs him, and ushers him to the centre of the barracks.

"Listen, okes. This Jimmy here is my buddy, and he's got the vokken kommandant licking his arse. If any of you are too thick to see why he's our ticket out of strife and vok him around, I'll sort you out."

Jimmy is a bit awed by this and says quietly to Kobus, "Hey, Kobus, you didn't have to do that."

Kobus claps him on the shoulder. "Do you think you are the only one who knows how to stand up for a friend?"

The rest of basics is more of the same, except Jimmy has a cohort of friends who do all the things he's useless at, except marching, for which there is no help. Even there, the sergeant undermines the korporaal's attempts at disciplining him. This easily makes up for the time he spends cooking for the kommandant, so everyone is happy except korporaal Riggs, who loses most of an intake's opportunities for bullying the softest target. His attempts at making up by picking on others fall apart because Kobus extends the new community spirit to making sure everyone's little weaknesses are covered, and no one dares argue with him. Johansen discovers he can get to sleep without smoking. Cloete's skill in ironing means he does more than his share, while Jimmy's floor cleaning proficiency relieves a few others of work, still leaving him pretty much nothing compared with the time he spent on bed making. All in all everyone's life is a little easier.

It's the day where the recruits volunteer for their future duties. Everyone knows the army tradition of getting the opposite to what you ask for but everyone nonetheless avidly hopes they make it to their choice and don't get the worst case, border duties – and the border these days seems to be somewhere in Angola. Jimmy knows he is going to the CSIR, and writes that in, then asks Kobus if he's planning on going to leadership school. Kobus looks shocked. "Buddy, do you really think I'm like one of those korporaal rats?"

"No, Kobus. People do what you tell them without bullying."

"No good. It's not the system. They would never let me do that."

"What about going for officer?"

"Never, not with my test scores."

"What then?"

"Someone has to go to the border."

"I'm not so sure of that. I mean we basically have a political problem here. If no one wanted to go to the border, the politicians would have to sort it out."

"Jislaaik. What are you, a whatchamacallit objectioner?"

"More like a coward. I knew they wouldn't send me out shooting if I had a CSIR job, so I didn't object to going to the army even though it's not the solution. I mean, we can't kill the entire black population, and calling it the border misses the point. It's not. It's happening in our own country. Soweto, Sebokeng."

Kobus took his hand. "Maybe you are right, maybe you are wrong. I'm not the guy who kicks korporaals in the balls, and I don't know vokkal about politics, but I am not going to run away from a fight. I'll keep my eyes open and think about it, hey. Even if you turn out to be a blerrie commie, you are still my buddy."

So it is that Kobus ends up going off to the war in Angola, and Jimmy goes back to the CSIR, this time wearing army brown.

5 Family

THE PRECEDENT OF NOOBY AND LUKAS having been set, Jimmy doesn't have to work hard for permission to stay in his own digs and the daily commute to the CSIR returns. Only the drab brown dress code and the occasional trip to military high command in the city to keep the paperwork in shape remind him he's still in the army.

Nooby's flat has one bedroom, a bathroom, a living room and a kitchen. Jimmy takes over Lukas's spot, a fold-down sleeper couch in the living room, surrounded by Lukas memorabilia, most of which Jimmy feels disinclined to explore.

The first morning, Jimmy wakes to the sound of an unfamiliar female voice. *Definitely not Mel.* A bad start to the day. He stumbles to the kitchen to make coffee, and nearly trips over Nooby, evidently on a similar mission. Nooby holds him at arms length. "Wassamatter, kid? Annoyed that I didn't introduce Nadine? I hardly know her better than I know you, met her in a bar last night." He inspects Jimmy more closely. "Or did they break you more than I thought at basics?"

Jimmy pushes him away, and they make unappetising

instant coffees in cool silence. As Nooby heads back to the bedroom, Jimmy pulls him back, nearly spilling his pair of coffees. "Sorry about that. Reminded me of something I'm trying to forget."

Nooby nods uncomprehendingly, and doesn't miss a step. Then stops and throws back at Jimmy: "Don't care if you prefer boys, more for me." Jimmy looks a bit scandalized, and Nooby gives up, closing the door a tad too forcefully. And that closes the subject.

Jimmy and Nooby settle into a routine, talking physics and otherwise mostly keeping out of each other's way.

Then after a few weeks, Jimmy's life changes unexpectedly. It's about eleven pm, and Jimmy is awake a bit later than usual when the phone rings. It's his mother. "Jimmy, your dad... the doctor thinks he may not make it through the night."

His mother is sounding really broken up, something new for him. "Ma, you didn't tell me he was unwell."

"You know how he is, never complains, doesn't think much of people who do. Something has obviously been bothering him for a while but he only went to the doctor last week, and obviously didn't get a proper diagnosis. He took pain killers until yesterday, when he collapsed and I had to call an ambulance. A specialist looked at him in hospital, and says he's pretty far gone. Bowel cancer."

"Ma, I'll try to get there as soon as I can."

He isn't sure how he's feeling. Mel pretty much burnt him out for grief, and what he feels now is a numbness, a certainty that he should be feeling something for his dad, but doesn't.

He looks for Nooby, but he's nowhere to be found,

probably out partying. Or spending the night with yet another girlfriend. He pulls out the phone directory. There must be hundreds of Smits in Pretoria, but only one has about the right initials, so he decides to take a chance, late as it is.

A sleepy voice answers.

"Is that Dr Smit, from the CSIR?"

"James! What are you doing phoning this time of night?"

"Dr Smit, it's my father. My mother thinks he won't make it through the night."

"I see. Look, I don't know if you can get a flight on such short notice, but if you can, just go. I will cover for you, but please phone me tomorrow to tell me what's happening."

The usual South African Airways booking office number is unattended so late at night. Jimmy manages to find a phone number for SAA at the airport, and it turns out there is a seat on an early morning flight. He explains why he needs it at short notice, suddenly finding he has emotions after all. The SAA clerk says, "Don't you worry, I'll book you on at National Serivice rates, and you can pay at the airport."

Jimmy is trying to work out how to get to the airport after all this, when Nooby walks in, looking a little unstable. "Wassamatter? Another bad girlfriend trip?"

Jimmy recovers his composure, wondering how Nooby has seen through him when he has said nothing about Mel, and explains.

Nooby sobers up fast. "That Smit is not a bad guy, all considered. Look, your flight is early enough that I can get you to the airport and be at the office in time. I'll let Smittie know, and you can give him a call once you know when you'll be heading back."

By ten the next morning, Jimmy is at Groote Schuur hospital, a huge edifice dominating the lower reaches of Table Mountain, just below Devil's Peak. His dad is in intensive care with tubes all over the place, barely conscious. But he recognises Jimmy, as he sits at the bedside, and wakes up enough to make a writing motion. Jimmy finds a piece of paper and pencil, and his dad writes in tenuous handwriting, "Proud of you son," and Jimmy holds his hand, nothing more to say. His mother is on the other side of the bed, holding the other hand. Jimmy stays there until the hand feels cold, and a nurse gently tells him and his mother it's all over.

Back at home, his mother gives him a hug. "Jimmy, your dad was never big on expressing emotion. That doesn't mean he didn't care. He was just of an age when people didn't talk about feelings."

"I know. But I wish he hadn't waited so long. It was hard to avoid the feeling that his work was all that mattered."

"What about you? You haven't told me much about life since that girl up and left you. There was the army, now this CSIR job. But don't you have any friends?"

"Ma, I actually had some good friends in the army, and the guy I'm sharing a flat with, who calls himself Nooby, isn't too bad."

He hesitates, wondering if he should share his older self story, but thinks better of it.

"But don't you have any girlfriends?"

"Ma, that's something I'm not so good at but give it time. I'm sure someone will show up."

"All I want is for you to be happy."

The next few days, he helps with the funeral arrangements. The will is very simple: his mother gets everything, with Jimmy next in line had she pre-deceased his dad. He walks about the very quiet house, fingering once-familiar furniture, the yellowwood dining room set, the overstuffed sofa, the oak headboard of his old bed.

It's a weirdly disconnected time. He's back in a past he's almost forgotten. He doesn't have too many happy memories. His mother always over-compensated for his dad's lack of affection, making him feel increasingly awkward as he grew up. His bookishness put off potential friends, and he spent many lonely hours reading in bed.

The funeral is attended by a few distant family members he barely remembers and a slew of his dad's work associates he doesn't know. It makes his dad seem even more a stranger. Time passes fast and Jimmy is in his mother's car on the way back to the airport. His dad's car, a Mercedes-Benz, sits shiny in the garage, waiting for its owner to return and drive it to the golf club, or wherever it should go next to sign up clients.

His mother looks so shrunken and insignificant as they share a last hug. It makes his whole concept of family very tenuous.

Two weeks later, an uncle he vaguely knows phones – possibly one who'd been at the funeral. Jimmy can't connect the voice and the name to a face. His mother has died overnight of a massive stroke. He gets leave for another funeral, and talks to the family lawyer about disposing of the estate. He doesn't want a house in Cape Town or a five-year-old Merc. He briefly entertains the idea of keeping his mother's more modest car, but decides not. *Mel is past. My family is past. Maybe I can make a new beginning. Put this money into long-term investments, then think about the future plan, how to get the money into Intel stocks and so on.*

His first night back in Pretoria, he feels a tingling in his head. Just as he starts to open an ornate envelope.

Are you bearing up OK?

As well as one does after losing both parents.

Right. I don't remember this as being as hard as some of the other things, but I thought I should check in anyway.

So just a brief house call this time?

More or less. A little reminder. Santa Cruz. Look for an opportunity to go there soon after you finish with the army. There could be obstacles on the way, but get there.

Something positive for a change. Nice. Meanwhile I just opened this thing, invitation to Mel's wedding. Should I go?

Up to you. My feeling at the time was I couldn't get more miserable.

I'll think about it. I'm not quite in the place you were.

One more thing: big financial crash of 2008. Whole countries go broke. Great time to buy Greek islands.

The presence is gone.

Next morning Jimmy remembers something and corners Nooby. "What did you mean, 'bad girlfriend trip'? You know, when I was going to see my dad before he died?"

"Ah. Every time you see me with a girl, you get a crazy depressed look on your face."

"Is that why you stopped bringing them home?"

"Could be. Do you want to talk about it?"

"No. Not now."

Nooby touches him on the shoulder. "Hard when you lose both your parents. Don't forget what friends are for."

6 Mastering the CSIR

L UKAS MEANWHILE IS SLOW to get his act together to move the rest of his stuff out, and keeps showing up in various states of altered consciousness. Jimmy doesn't ask but he suspects stronger narcotics than he's ever encountered. On one of these visits, Jimmy has a paper on quantum entanglement he's been trying to make sense of. Nooby takes a quick look at the paper and retires to the couch for a snooze. Jimmy goes to the kitchen to make a cup of tea and returns to find Lukas has shown up and is glancing at the paper casually.

"Spot anything interesting?" Jimmy asks.

"They should have used Lebesgue integration. Shorten the paper to two lines."

Nooby wakes up and grins. "Forget the hippy look. This guy would have three PhDs by now if he gave a shit."

Lukas grunts, gets his things together and leaves.

"Is he always like this?" Jimmy makes a note to look up Lebesgue integration.

"Ah, you caught him in a good mood. Probably had a good trip."

"What a waste."

Nooby shrugs and goes back to sleep.

Coming out on a conscript salary is something else but, as promised, Dr Smit knows the dodges. A month after Jimmy's mother died, he calls Jimmy into his office.

"James, my lad, when did you last take a holiday?"

"I don't know, some time in undergrad, I went to visit the folks in Cape Town."

"Oh yes, pleasurable, I take it?"

Jimmy finds himself opening up in a way that surprises him. "My dad was always so busy, selling his life policies, that I didn't get to see much of him. I wasn't so close to my mother those days, so I mostly tried to get out of the house. I took the train to Muizenberg every good beach day. On bad beach days, I went into the city or took walks around the mountain, and once or twice took the train to Stellenbosch when there was nothing else to do."

"Not so excited with Stellenbosch? The hub of Afrikaner culture?"

"I'm sorry, a bit starchy for my liking. I was interested in seeing the wine farms, but all the ones close to town charge for tasting to deter the students, and I was deterred." He grins, wondering where this is leading. Smit hasn't been all that chummy in general, notwithstanding his sensitive handling of Jimmy's loss of his parents.

"Anyway James, to business. The CSIR has an extremely long-running project in Margate, an electronic shark barrier. Some are saying it will never work, others that we should keep it going for the research value. I think it would do some good to have a completely neutral person give it a once-over, and thoroughly evaluate it with no prejudice."

"Who, me? I don't think I know much about the subject."

"Neither do the politicians who are funding us, and the chappies on the ground need to be able to explain themselves to a non-expert. And besides –" he winks "– S & T."

"S & T?"

"Subsistence and travel. I can make sure you get paid a good rate. It will help out with the budget a bit, I'm sure. But once you get back, write me a report, then do some decent hard work to make up. OK?"

"Thank you Dr Smit. When do I go?"

"The storm season should be about over by the end of September, so I suggest we send you out for the first two weeks of October. That should also miss the school holiday crowds."

Jimmy walks out of the office elated. *Margate! A Capetonian generally doesn't go to the Natal coast for holidays, when what we have is so* superior. The attitude sickens him. *But with ma and dad to visit for free you play along. Cape Town is nice enough but what's wrong with slumming a bit for a change?* He almost walks into Nooby.

"Yo! Wassamatter? Fallen in love? Oh, yeah, forgot. You don't do love. Fallen in depression again?" Nooby grins.

For an instant Jimmy's elation flickers and he forces a Mel thought down. "Smit's sending me to Margate. Report on the electronic shark barrier."

"Ah, scoring some S & T. Good for you. What kind of report?"

"Uh, an unbiased one, from an outsider, not a specialist."

"I can tell you now why the barrier won't work."

"Oh?"

"Marine engineers. They have no marine engineers on the project. You need damn good insights into the chemistry of the ocean, how tides rip things around and so on to build anything that stands a chance of lasting down there. The people on the job are jumped-up techies with broeder connections."

"Right, then. I'll write that up at the end of the trip and have a nice time on the beach."

"I wouldn't if I were you. Find out what Smit really wants when you get back, then write the report."

Margate. Johannesburg by the sea in summer, a quiet sleepy hollow the rest of the year. The CSIR puts him up in cheap accommodation – the only kind out of season – near the beach. He contemplates whether he has to wear his military garb, and decides against it. *Easier to ask forgiveness than permission, and anyway there's no military personnel in the local CSIR group.* He changes into civvies and wanders down to the beach where the project personnel are making a fine effort at looking busy, with a 4×4 and lots of ropes sprawling around the sands. He walks up to them. "Dr Smit sent me here."

One of them looks up. "Ah, the executioner." Jimmy looks puzzled, and the person who addressed him strides towards him, sunburnt face hiding behind impressive whiskers, a safari suit a bit out of place on the beach. "This project has had a pretty good run and when a person we didn't request shows up, we can be pretty sure someone is thinking of winding it up."

Jimmy tries to look impassive but the fellow laughs. "I'm

Tiedemann. Kevin Tiedemann. I run this show, after a fashion. Look, it's not your fault what head office thinks. If you really want to find out what's happening, chip in with the work, and you'll also get some nice free time on the beach."

It turns out there isn't a whole lot for him to do. The cable is in the sea, as are various instruments, and time on the beach is really where it's at. That night he finds himself in a dive called the Palm Grove, almost empty but for some school kids flouting the liquor laws, and a few waiters obviously happy for some out of season custom, licit or no. There's live music, but not very good, obviously a filler band for the dead season. It gets very smokey even with a small clientele, and he gets out by 9pm, and wanders around the town. There isn't very much to see: a building tantalisingly labelled **The Casino**, which turns out to be a movie theatre, the usual sprinkling of small-town shops and a fair number of touristy-looking shops and hotels. He finds his way back to his room and falls asleep, wondering how he will fill the time.

The next couple of weeks he lives frugally, taking in a few movies and catching up on reading, while pretending to work with the CSIR crew, who are also pretending to work, so he fits right in. His best break is talking to the professional lifesavers, who give him an even more detailed breakdown than Nooby's on why the whole thing will never work. And better still, give him some hot hints on how to surf.

Back in Pretoria, he arrives home to find Nooby for once at home without a girlfriend.

"What's the matter? Did you get bored with sex? Or did you remember Mr Depressive was heading back?"

Nooby grins. "Well, every now and then a guy needs a

break. And I'm working on a paper that's starting to look good. You look pretty tanned up. Did you find out anything useful?"

"Yeah, well the guys who maintain the good old fashioned shark nets think the project doesn't have a hope in hell of working. The electronics are too delicate to survive long in the ocean so you need the shark nets in anyway for backup. Makes it all pointless."

"Well anyway, like I said, find out what Smit really wants before you write your report. Like to go out for a change? I'm bored with getting this paper together, and you need to show off your tanned bod and pick up some talent just this once."

They head for a bar and Nooby monopolises the conversation on the way. "You'll never guess what happened to Lukas. Failed his security clearance. So, now wait for it, they said he couldn't work at CSIR any more and sent him off to military HQ. Where, and this is the good bit, his job is copying top secret documents."

"Top secret?"

"Exactimo. And this because he failed his security clearance. Anyway to add insult to injury, after a week of this, the CO called him in and accused him of not taking enough pride in his work."

Nooby parks outside a bar, and they walk in, still sniggering at the idiocy of the military. After one beer, Jimmy is looking queasy. Nooby checks him out. "I didn't know you couldn't handle your booze."

"It's not that, it's the smoke. I can drink four, five beers easy, without feeling sick, but in a smokey bar, just one is enough to make me want to throw up."

"Can't have that. Let's go home and have some beers where you can enjoy them. No hot babes here anyway."

Jimmy isn't sure why he's told Nooby his beer limits, because it turns into something of a contest, the consequences of which are still slowing him down when Dr Smit invites him into his office the next morning.

"Well, James, before you submit your written report, I would like your informal impressions."

Without thinking, Jimmy (or possibly last night's beer) says, "Dr Smit, we all know why the project is a flop. You need marine engineers in that environment. What do we want the official line to be?"

Dr Smit laughs, before Jimmy comprehends that he may have said the wrong thing. "Bright lad." He leans forward. "Listen, people in the know don't believe that apartheid can last much longer. What we have to do in the CSIR is make sure we are the premier science agency in the country, so whatever comes after depends on us. Officially, if any project fails, it fails because the best talent in the country tried and it failed because we don't have the capacity in the country to do it. We never fail because we tried the wrong approach."

Jimmy's head is clearing fast. "And all that talk we hear of various delegations visiting the ANC and how bad they are to talk to terrorists? Am I to guess right that some of those delegations are close to the corridors of power?"

Smit shakes his hand. "I knew you would fit right in. Not a word of this now. Look, if you can get me the report in a week or so, that will be all right. Meanwhile, I've been wondering if you should talk to Professor Barnardus in the Tukkies Physics department about doing your M. We want to increase the number of higher degrees here, and you had a good Honours, so you should do all right."

"Dr Smit, I don't know what the professor works on, but I'm happy to talk to him. Do you think the Afrikaans universities will also be on the right side of a new system, I mean, the places like Wits with all their protests and so on. . . "

Smit laughs. "Don't worry lad. A new government will want to be a going concern, and all the institutions that currently have good connections to government will carry right on."

Jimmy walks out of the office in a daze. *Incredible. Seems older me was right about that. Let's see how it actually pans out. Will Africa's oldest liberation movement really get conned so easily?*

That night Jimmy sounds out Nooby. Nooby looks thoughtful. "I don't know much about Barnardus, but what I do know isn't that great, but it shouldn't be a big disaster if you do your masters with him. It's a PhD that really counts anyway. I say keep the bosses happy as long as you want to stay here." He grins. "Another beer?"

Jimmy groans and shakes his head.

A week or so later, Jimmy is visiting Barnardus at the University of Pretoria campus. Barnardus is stiff and formal, and wears a jacket and tie, even though the weather is tending towards the warm end of spring. He invites Jimmy in and points stiffly at a stiff upright chair.

"A Wits graduate, eh."

"Yes, professor. I brought my Honours thesis in." He hands it over and Barnardus makes a showing of paging through it.

"I'm sure this is good work. Now I have an M graduate by the name of Jakobus Pietersen, who has just been accepted for a PhD at University of California in Santa Cruz, and we have been talking about filling in some of the gaps between his M and his new PhD project. Over there they have to do courses for a while before the PhD really starts, so he can use some help to keep going." Barnardus leans forward. "I'll give you some of his work to study and if you can make sense of it and identify an area to work on, we'll let Pietersen know." He hands over a bound volume and a few papers. "Here. If you can get back to me next week, and let me know what you can do, we can take it from there."

Santa Cruz? Now where have I heard that before? Could that future self thing have been for real, not some sort of psychotic episode? He brings himself back to the here and now, and thanks Barnardus for the materials.

That night Jimmy and Nooby work through the Pietersen thesis and the papers. "Well," says Nooby after a couple of hours, "I think Pietersen knows his stuff. But of course Barnardus has stuck his name on all the papers. Did he say much about the detail to you?"

"No, not a word."

"Wouldn't be surprised if it's above him. Probably another broeder. Not that everyone at Tukkies is useless. The broeders stick out like sore thumbs."

"What about the Santa Cruz angle? Any way I can get leverage from that? I'd like to go somewhere more exotic than Margate some time."

"I doubt you can go there until you finish your two years, but you should try to angle for a trip there afterwards. I've been looking for places to do a postdoc. I'll have a chat with Pietersen, see if he has any ideas. This quantum entanglement stuff is right up my street."

"And mine," adds Jimmy, still wondering how all this connects with his older self's past – and whether his timeline is changed somehow by his older self's intervention.

The next week, Barnardus signs Jimmy up for his Masters. Pietersen and Nooby start a regular correspondence, with Jimmy chipping in where he can. Barnardus, true to Nooby's prediction, lets them get on with it. Nooby extends his letter-writing to a Santa Cruz professor who is at first pleased with his insightful questions. Then Nooby asks if there's a postdoc going for after he gets out of the army, and there's a long silence. He writes a letter to Pietersen, and Pietersen replies: "Don't talk to anyone here about the army. Did you forget about sanctions?" Pietersen manages to patch things up for Nooby on the basis that he's not real army but an unwilling conscript. So Nooby lands himself a postdoc in California, due to start after he's taken a break to recover from the military.

Momentum starts to build. Jimmy meets Barnardus weekly, and has regular chats with Nooby about the detail. Lukas occasionally drops in and on the rare occasions when he isn't high takes a casual glance at whatever they are working on and disposes of a tough problem with an offhand remark. A few months later, Barnardus at a regular meeting tells Jimmy: "I have a sabbatical coming up and I've asked Pietersen if he can arrange for me to visit. I will be happy to put in a good word with Dr Smit so you can go with me. It will be second half of next year, so you should be out of the army by then. It should be an excellent experience for you, if you would like to join me."

Jimmy nods enthusiastically. *And Nooby might be there too. If he gets his act together.*

All goes well at first. Even the depressing memory – *stupid, stupid, I knew it was pointless to go* – of attending Mel's wedding quickly fades with interesting work to keep Jimmy occupied, and the prospect of the first big step on his world-changing journey looming. At each meeting, Barnardus adds to his stock of stories about professors he will meet at Santa Cruz, as well as plans for travelling around the state. But after about a month of increasing enthusiasm, his mood is very different. As Jimmy enters the office, Barnardus closes the door, stoney-faced. "What's the matter professor?"

"Someone has told the professors in Santa Cruz that I have military connections, and they are withdrawing the invitation."

Nooby. Jimmy is certain of it. *Who else? But he's not even there yet. Why would he risk causing chaos when he could end up getting tangled in it? Makes no kind of sense.*

7 Signifying

NOOBY IS AT HOME when Jimmy gets back. There's a surprise: Lukas is there too, looking very jolly, not his usual self at all. Jimmy wonders briefly what this is about, but gets right to the point.

"Hey, Lukas. Nooby, I have a question for you."

Nooby raises an eyebrow.

"Nooby, don't go all innocent on me. We're on the same side on this. Did you sabotage Barnardus's sabbatical?"

"Who, me?" If the innocence is feigned, he's good.

Jimmy notices Lukas is looking at his feet, even more withdrawn than usual, geniality suddenly gone. Jimmy fixes him with a glare. "OK, I think I know who did it. I can see why you'd sabotage him, but what about me?"

Nooby grins. "Well anyway, whoever did it did him a service. He would be out of his depth in a physics department where they don't defer to broeders."

Lukas looks up, his eyes doing strange things. "Sorry, man. I didn't really think of you. That guy was a real creep when I did undergrad, that's why I quit Tukkies and went to Wits. No regrets. Learnt some great physics and did some great drugs."

Jimmy tries to fix him in eye contact and gives up. "Well, what are you on now?"

"Not on, coming down from. You ever tripped on acid? LSD? Crazy stuff. You look at your nose, and suddenly it's reaching down to the floor."

Lukas is babbling incoherently and Jimmy can't take it. This idiot has wrecked a big step in his older self's plan. "I can get voices in my head without any damn chemicals. Listen to you, you're a bloody genius and you're pickling your brain."

"You are getting what now?" Lukas's eyeballs are looking a bit more under control as he turns them on Jimmy, who has a sinking feeling but somehow it all pours out. The flashes in his head, the future self, the plausible-sounding predictions of the future, how Santa Cruz was supposed to be a big opportunity.

"Jeez," says Nooby. "And there was I thinking you only had girlfriend problems. Look at Lukas: he's found love and he's a transformed dude."

Jimmy grins awkwardly. "I have a thousand years of misery to look forward to, it seems, and no easy way out like that. Which seems pretty extreme. Are you going to call the guys in the white coats now? And what's that about Lukas finding love? I thought Lukas was only cheerful because he trashed Barnardus's plans." He wonders what sounds crazier: the future self, or his inability to get over Mel. To these guys, probably Mel.

Lukas is looking thoughtful. "So this is why you're struggling through all that quantum entanglement garbage.

Oh, yeah, the girlfriend effect is real enough, but we can talk about that any time. Tell me more."

"Well, my older self eventually figured out how to use it to talk to me and I would like the option to get in ahead of him."

"In a different timeline. You can't rescue yourself. That's if the older you has this right. How long exactly did you say it took him to work it all out?"

Jimmy felt cold. "About a thousand years."

"Jeez, I thought you were a bit slow but not *that* slow."

They all laugh. "Look," Lukas goes on, "why not leave this to the pros, and get on with your other projects. What were they? Saving the world and living forever?"

"You mean you don't think I'm crazy?"

"Maybe you are, maybe not, but working this out for sure beats getting high. First a hot girl, now a hot physics problem. Who says luck goes in threes? Two is enough for me. And don't worry too much about Santa Cruz. Once you are out of the army, we'll work something out."

They talk well into the night, Lukas's pathetic revenge on Barnardus a distant memory. In the end, Lukas is too tired to go home, and goes to sleep on the floor, sleeping the fractured sleep of withdrawal.

Jimmy wakes up with a terrible feeling that he's handed the future of the world, no, not just the world, but possibly all possible universes, to a junkie. He trips his way out of his bed (literally) and Lukas has gone. He makes himself some coffee, obviously not too quietly because Nooby appears bleary-eyed. "Wassup? Waking the dead?"

"Sorry, woke up a bit clumsy. Where did Lukas go?"

"Home I suppose. You worrying he'll turn out the mad scientist and use your older you's ideas to wreck the universe?"

"Well. . ."

"Don't worry yourself. Under the hippy junkie persona Lukas is the sanest person I know. He only rejects reality to the extent that it rejects him. Give me some of that coffee."

Over the next few weeks, Lukas drops in at random intervals, mutters something about some new area of physics he's exploring and disappears again. Jimmy wonders how he's going down at military HQ. "Not taking enough pride in his work," he says out aloud, not realising Nooby is standing right behind him.

Nooby bashes him on the shoulder. "Listen to you! The army has inserted some of its DNA into you."

I wonder if older me would be shocked at this development. Seems to me Lukas may just signify, *whatever that means.*

Meanwhile life goes on. One day Smit calls him into his office again. "James, you remember that report you wrote me on the shark barrier? The higher-ups were very impressed. We have another project not going so well, and it's also not your speciality, but you may know a bit more about it."

"Wield the hatchet again on your behalf?"

"I wouldn't put it so crudely. But yes. We have a group who've latched onto some parallel computing hardware called transputers, apparently not spelt with a capital letter. Anyway the claim is that they can make supercomputers for much less money and not worry about sanctions, but their big project, weather prediction, isn't going very far."

"Well I can't promise, but if it involves days on the beach, I can do it." Jimmy grins, forgetting he's talking to a mostly humourless broeder. But Smit rises to the occasion.

"Lad, I appreciate that you like to have fun, but don't let the people on the project see you laughing at them. Strictly between you and me."

Jimmy leaves the office with the feeling that this group is less favoured by the higher ups, and decides to be as fair as possible. Anyway if he's to be there long-term, a reputation for being the broeders' hatchet man isn't how he wants to be seen.

The transputer group turns out mostly to be physicists. They have diligently converted FORTRAN code over to the transputer's very particular model of parallel coding, but it achieves very little speedup, to the extent that a latest-technology plain vanilla UNIX box would probably be faster. He spends a week talking to them and working through their code. In the end the difficulty seems rather obvious. The assumption of the hardware designers that you can break a program down into dozens of independent parts doesn't really fit the problem. There is too much communication between the independent parts. He changes a few details so the program runs on only 4 processors instead of 16 and it runs faster. This time he writes the report carefully explaining the limitations of the technology and how it is not the best fit to the problem, hoping he hasn't made the researchers look like complete dolts.

As this is going on, Lukas has disappeared, but Nooby assures Jimmy that he's working on their problem and will surface in his own good time.

Life settles into a pattern: Nooby winding down his CSIR activities while looking for post-army recreational opportunities, Jimmy champing at the bit making slow progress on his Masters and Lukas – true to prediction – making occasional appearances with pronouncements that leave the others mystified. But it feels like progress. And Lukas is happy, so the risk of the whole thing being in the hands of a flake eases and Jimmy starts to enjoy life – even if he still has Mel moments to fight off.

Then the whole world turns upside down.

8 Santa Cruz Liberation

JAN Smuts, the one non-National Party prime minister whose name graces an airport. Jimmy wonders what he would think of today's world. A relatively liberal figure for his time, author of the preamble to the UN Charter, a philosopher, but nonetheless locked into the world view that Blacks were not entitled to full rights. His liberalism only extended really to rapprochement between Boer and Brit. Now Mandela is free, will this airport name stick? Or will it go in a sweep of name changes?

Free Mandela day: he thinks back to the surreal event. Half of the CSIR is crammed into the multimedia room. Nothing seems to be happening for a long time and an Afrikaans voice is dwelling on the weather as if at a quiet moment in a sports commentary. Then this rather uncertain-looking old man steps out into history, not quite sure if he belongs, and tentatively puts his fist in the air. He belongs. There's the crazy drive to Cape Town, the people along the road waving him on, many of whom not that long ago, if they thought of him at all, thought of him as a terrorist. Then the halting but firm speech in Cape Town, making it clear that the armed struggle was still on, finally exhorting the crowds to discipline, so no one can say we can't control our own people.

Jimmy looks around in astonishment. His conservative broeder colleagues have all found a new love, all but hugging each other in excitement. He finds his way back to the office, wondering if much work will get done that day. He sits back, oblivious to all the technology around him, trying to make sense of it all, when the phone rings.

"James, did you see that?" It's Barnardus.

"Yes, professor."

"Remarkable. I've just had a phone call from Pietersen. He's been watching along with some of the professsors, and it seems, all of a sudden, we are welcome in Santa Cruz."

"Oh. So your sabbatical may be on after all?"

"I certainly hope so. Listen, talk to Dr Smit. Assume it's on, and work out how much time the CSIR will pay for you to go with me. If there's any problem, let me know. They owe me a few favours. Let's show those Americans what a good South African professor and his student can do. Let's not wait. I'm sure I can advance my sabbatical by a semester for an opportunity like this." Barnardus is so keen, he's bordering on incoherent. Jimmy can almost see him flapping at the other end of the line.

Jimmy slowly lowers the phone. He decides to give Nooby a call. Nooby picks up on the tenth ring, just as Jimmy was about to give up. "I thought you weren't there."

"Well I'm not sure entirely where I am. I may be on a different planet. Did you see the Mandela thing? Crazy stuff. Why did they put a sports commentator on?"

"I don't know if he usually does sports. I think more

like, he didn't know whether to praise Mandela or go with the usual terrorist line. Anyway, Barnardus says his invitation to Santa Cruz is on again, and is super keen for me to tag along. Why would he want me there so desperately?"

"Possibly because he's bloody clueless and needs you for backup? Do you want me to find you some contacts once I get there?"

"Please. If we don't get there before you. We were supposed to get there a bit after you start, but Barnardus would jump on a plane today if he could. We may even beat you to it."

Things move fast from there. After being increasingly isolated, South Africa rejoins the academic community of scholars just as a thing called the Internet is starting to spread across academia, and Pietersen is suddenly a whole lot closer than a round trip by airmail, even if South African connections start out slow and unreliable.

So here Jimmy is two months on, at the airport, heading out to UC Santa Cruz, to work with real scientists who haven't been constrained by living in a pariah state. Perfect, except for being in the company of a troglodyte. And getting there ahead of Nooby, without the benefit of a smart scout to set things up.

He and Prof Barnardus edge forward in the queue to check in. They arrive at the front, and drag their luggage through to the check-in counter. Barnardus is still visibly excited. "You know, I didn't think freeing Mandela would affect me so. I mean, all those years not being totally welcome overseas."

They pass over their passports and tickets.

"Are the two of you travelling together?" The check-in lady flicks her eyes from the one to the other, as she pages through their tickets. She types endlessly on the keyboard. "Let's see now. Professor, with your frequent flier gold status, we are a bit crowded in economy and we would normally offer you a free upgrade to business, but we only have one seat left."

Barnardus eyes Jimmy out expectantly. He takes the hint. "Go on prof. Let them upgrade you. I can handle cramped seating OK."

They go through the security check point in silence.

"Thank you James. You would probably think me rude if I went to the business class lounge after this."

"No, no. Go. When I'm a professor I'll get all the perks."

The professor smiles gratefully, and takes his briefcase in the direction of the business class lounge.

Jimmy grins gormlessly after him, then drops the expression as he turns away. *Probably boring company anyway.* He wanders around the duty free and, aside from some export-only wines, wonders what the point is: everything seems pretty pricey, duty free or no. He finds his paperback in his backpack and settles in for a read, not paying much attention to the other passengers. The flight is called, and he joins the scrummage to the boarding gate. Finally, he is at his seat, finds a pen in his pack in case he gets around to doing the crosswords, stows his newspaper in the magazine pocket, and drops his book on his window seat. Despite the full flight, his row is empty. *Professor could have sat here anyway. Probably buttering up the good customers. Good for me, elbow room. Maybe a lie down.*

He sits down, hefting the paperback out of the way, and buckles his belt. He finds the safety card, and reads it, not expecting too much exciting. But still, someone took the trouble. The last few passengers are boarding, and someone plonks down in the aisle seat. She has a duty free bag, and shoves it into the magazine pocket. He looks her way, not taking in much. "Looks like they're closing the door. Maybe we'll be lucky and not be crowded out here," he mumbles in her general direction.

"Mmph," she says, not paying too much attention.

He alternates between reading and noting the various routines pre take-off: the safety demo, the warnings to buckle up and not smoke until the signs go out, and only then in the smoking section. "Yeah, right, makes as much sense as a peeing and non-peeing section of a swimming pool." His neighbour shows no sign of interest. He returns to his book, stopping to look out as the plane accelerates down the runway, marvelling at how such a big thing can leap into the air – laws of physics or no. Then they are clear of the airport, climbing through the brown haze that passes for air in Joburg.

After a meaningless meal that doesn't fit departure or arrival time zones, things settle for the night. The cabin crew clear his tray, and blinds go down around the cabin. He feels something prod his thigh, and turns to his neighbour to find she's lying across her seat and the empty one between. *Oh well, no worse than if the prof was sitting there.* Once the cabin crew have cleared the rest of the cabin, he feels the need to take a leak and somehow contrives to climb over his recumbent neighbour without stepping on her. He finds his way back and she's gone, no doubt also using the facilities. He dusts his clothes, as if this will expunge the disgusting reek of tobacco that follows him from the back of the plane, more persistent than the stale urine essence of the toilet cubical. As he pushes past her seat, he brushes against her duty-free bag in the seat pocket and sees what's inside. A bottle. He sits down and peers at it more closely, not noticing she's back.

"Stealing my duty free are you?"

He looks up feeling a vivid shade of scarlet washing across his face. "Uh, no, just happened to read the label."

"And you like what you see?"

"Well, no, I don't like scotch," he says reflexively.

"You will like Chivas," she says, opening the bottle. Their eyes lock.

9   Dianne

A FEW WEEKS INTO the Santa Cruz visit, Jimmy's wondering what he's doing there. Although Nooby emails regularly and points him at contacts and Pietersen is happily doing his courses, Jimmy is starting to wonder if physics really is his field. Whenever he runs into a hard problem, an email to Lukas results in a quick fix, often embarrassingly simple. *Shouldn't have let Lukas take charge. How am I going to get into a PhD programme if I don't have any good ideas?* He wanders into seminars, talks to professors and students, discovers the pleasures of Internet newsgroups, goes to the library, yet can't get focussed.

Newsgroups are a great way of discussing with like-minded people but have an infuriating habit of collapsing into flame wars when someone says something that annoys someone else. *So I wonder how this Internet gets to be really big. I can't see non-tech people using this. But email on a decent speed network is great compared with the primitive thing we have back home. Could be some marketing genius gets hold of that.*

Meanwhile Barnardus is fussing around, taking people

out for lunch, going to as many social occasions as he can, and generally avoiding talking technical detail – unless he can repeat something he heard from someone else. This, Jimmy decides, is the real killer for him. In the first week, he tells Barnardus a few things he's picked up, and next thing Barnardus is repeating the exact words as his own. *Jeez, I have a parrot supervising my Masters.*

He is walking around the campus, trying to make sense of all this, and to find an angle to get remotivated, when he starts thinking of Mel again. *This is getting me nowhere. Got to find a distraction.* He spots a notice advertising a party for incoming international graduate students that night, and decides to crash it.

The party is in progress by the time he gets there, and he hasn't shaken the Mel mood. He spots an attractive-looking female student just as she looks his way and favours him with the tight smile of unintended eye contact. *So much for moving on.* Then he feels the familiar sensation in his head. *What now? I don't get you every time I think of Mel and this doesn't feel like a crisis.*

Yet. I'll stay with you. The party has some rough moments but you get a real opportunity.

Which you took.

Which I missed.

He shakes his head as if to clear it, and finds a drink. A professor is standing near. "Hi, I'm Phil Ridler. Did I see you around the Physics department?"

"Yes. I'm visiting from South Africa, working on a Masters, maybe could be interested in a PhD."

The friendly smile vanishes. "Ah, you're with the racist

professor."

"Barnardus? Sorry, I am not entirely in his camp. I just got sucked into working with him because I wasn't brave enough to go to jail rather than go into the army."

"Draft dodgers are also known to flee the country, you know. They did that here during Vietnam."

"Easy for you to say when you don't have friends and family to think of. And anyway, I'm pretty astonished at how Barnardus has suddenly decided that Mandela is his greatest hero, let alone the way he is suddenly welcome here. I've read a lot of history of the anti-apartheid movement, but he's only grown up on propaganda about how evil the so-called terrorists were."

"Do you think that change is for real?"

"Who knows? As long as it translates to a just society I'm happy. Sadly, revolutionary movements all too often end up looking like what they fought against, like *Animal Farm*."

"Look, I need to talk to the real incoming students. I'm sorry if I prejudged you but I have reason to be suspicious of sudden converts. Would you like to meet me tomorrow some time? Talk to my secretary."

Jimmy nods. The professor hands over a card and leaves him, and Jimmy wanders around, grabbing snacks and drinks. *That wasn't so hard to handle. Is there more?*

Actually the bit I remember was getting stuck on thinking about Mel.

Thanks. Maybe you are helping a bit with that after all. So what's the big opportunity?

Stick around until the party thins out. See who's the last one left with you. Shouldn't be long. I'll stay with you.

Starts well, let's try to make it go better than my timeline.

The party gradually thins down until Jimmy and a friendly-looking girl are the only ones left. They approach awkwardly. He grins, remembering his older self's prediction, and that breaks the ice. Her response is a fair number of degrees warmer than the one from early in the party.

"Hi," she says. "Party broke up pretty quick. What are you planning to work on for your PhD? I'm supposed to be helping out with making international students feel at home, so I hope you're international."

"I'm actually just visiting, but I'm interested in physics, quantum entanglement. Doing a Masters. Scouting out PhD options."

"I'm in biology. Have you heard of the human genome project?"

"I'm not sure –"

"It's a giant project to sequence the entire human genome, 3-billion base pairs. It should be done in ten to fifteen years but in the meantime there's a lot going on in related projects. Some people are saying biology will eventually be a branch of computer science because of all the computation this will involve, so I'm taking some CS courses."

"I did some CS in undergrad. Maybe we should talk more about where this is all going."

"Why not? And I hope you aren't here only for work. What do you do for fun?"

Jimmy is about to say, I don't have fun because I don't have a life when there is a voice in his head shrieking, ***don't don't don't don't say it don't***. He opens and closes his mouth, shakes his head, and says, "Excuse me – hold that thought –

gotta go to the bathroom." He rushes to the toilet, wondering how he remembered under that sort of pressure to use the Americanism for toilet. Once in a cubicle, he asks, *What the hell was that about?*

In the same situation, I said something like I don't have a life, and she kind of reflexively said something snide, and we lost the moment.

Like me rushing off to the bathroom?

Get the hell back before it's too late.

He does, and she's still there, and looks at him with concern. "Are you OK?"

"Yes, I forgot lunch, and felt a bit weak after drinks on too little food. Speaking of which, how about some decent food?"

"Like what?"

"I make a pretty good pesto. And I think we aren't too late to buy ingredients, though it's a bit of a walk to the shops."

"Make pesto? Why bother when you can get it from a bottle?"

"Let me show you." He suddenly realises he doesn't know her name. "I'm Jimmy." He offers her his hand.

She takes it. "Dianne. And I have a car, so we can get to the shops quickly."

"Jimmy and Dianne. Sounds like a comedy duo." She grins and takes his arm, leading him to her car.

They get back from the shops and she is still chuckling at his pronunciation. "When you said you liked bah-zil I thought you had to be gay. *Bay-sil.*"

He leads her in to his apartment. "I'll show you who's gay," and gives her a deep searching kiss. "Seconds?"

She grins. "Yes please. Then show me what you can make that's better than pesto out of a bottle."

As he's pounding the garlic, leaves and cheese, he says, "I should really make the pasta fresh too, but too much effort for a small amount and without a machine." He meanwhile adds linguine to boiling water, and goes back to pounding, this time adding pine nuts.

"Fresh pasta? Now you're trying to impress me."

"Not yet. Taste first. Can you open the wine?" It's a California chardonnay. The local store has nothing from South Africa. He adds olive oil to the pesto and, as the pasta gets close to done, a couple of spoons of the cooking water.

As they sit down to the pasta he says, "You were telling me what you do for fun."

"Oh yes... this is delicious!"

"Better than out of a bottle?"

"I take it all back. So, fun... My dad introduced me to piloting a light plane. Beats long-distance driving for speed and you get to see everything from above. And anyway, I asked *you* what you do for fun. Obviously cooking. What else?"

"I'm not so big on heights myself. I like to explore things closer to the ground. I grew up in Cape Town in South Africa, and there are great walks around the mountain. Table Mountain – named for its flat top."

"South Africa! I was going to ask about the accent. How are things now Mandela is free?"

"In some ways great, but there's some ugly violence from groups who won't accept change."

"And you? How do you feel about the change?"

He tells her of his experience of reading up on the ANC, being drafted to the army, trying to avoid a combat role and somehow getting sucked into the broeders' circle – the broeders needing a fair amount of explanation.

"So do you have a future in the new South Africa?"

"I don't know. I am naturally inclined to support those who want change but have a horrible feeling that the inner circle of the old order will find a way to pull the strings. I suppose if I can do a PhD overseas I can get a bit of perspective, but I'm not doing too well with finding an area of physics I can work with."

"What else can you do?"

"Well, like I said, I did do some CS, but only undergrad."

"Why don't you talk to the biology people too? They may be interested in CS grads with a general science background. There's a lot of new stuff going on there, and too few biologists who know CS to do it all, and too few CS grads with biology for them to be picky."

The next day, he makes an appointment to see Ridler, and goes with Dianne to see her advisor, Ed Brookfield. Dianne introduces them, and most of the conversation is around her project, which Jimmy finds depressingly obscure. Brookfield at the end of the discussion with Dianne asks: "Well, Jimmy, are you just a sightseer, or are you also planning on doing a PhD?"

"Professor, I'm supposed to be looking for a topic in physics, but nothing really grabs me. I've heard there's demand for people with a little computer science background in biology, but I know nothing about biology." He makes a mental note to email Lukas for an update on the physics project, to make sure it's in safe hands, if he commits this early to switching focus to biology. *Anyway, isn't that the order things went with older me? And without a Lukas or even Nooby for backup?*

"That's not an obstacle. The main thing is you need good GRE scores, and you can catch up on missing material in your courses. Normally you would have to do both a general and a biology subject test, but you could make a case for substituting CS. How much background do you have in large-scale computation?"

"GRE?" Jimmy feels like a dolt: he is sure this is something he should know.

Dianne explains. "Standard test. US universities don't trust each other so we have to do this thing to get into grad school."

Jimmy nods. "I think Nooby may have said something about that." He now has to explain who Nooby is, then goes on: "I have worked on weather models, but the hardware we had was a dog to program, and I was only brought onto the project because they were failing."

"Did you fix the problem?" Brookfield asks.

"Not really, but I explained why they were failing."

"That's something I suppose. Have you talked to any computational groups while you've been lurking around physics?"

"No, but I'm seeing Prof Ridler this afternoon, and maybe he can point me at the right people."

"Ridler? Not sure if I know what he does but I have an idea he may be doing something computational. Anyway try to get in with a computational group while you're here. Demonstrated capability in large-scale computation especially working with someone we know will stand you in good stead."

After the meeting, Dianne says, "Ed is generally pretty good at sizing up potential. If he thinks you may be good, he'll help you hit the right buttons on the admissions process."

"Thanks. I'm seeing Ridler after lunch."

They arrange to meet up afterwards.

Ridler is a bit wary at the start of the conversation, but warms to Jimmy as he shares anecdotes of life under the final years of apartheid. Then they get to business. "Professor, I was wondering if anyone here is doing anything in computation. I was involved at the tail end of a weather modelling project, but only really to tell them why their approach wouldn't work."

"Weather modelling? We have a group doing something in that space, and they've just bought a big SGI. Got a good deal: Silicon Graphics is trying to break out of the pure graphics space. Trouble is, our guys don't have much experience in programming one of these beasts. Would you like an intro to them?"

"Thanks. Should I check in with you again tomorrow?"

"I have a few meetings, so probably a better bet to give me a couple days. I generally read my email fairly quickly, so send me a reminder if you don't hear from me."

"Thanks, professor." As Jimmy leaves, he remembers something. "Professor, why were you so suspicious of me at the start?"

"I had a grad student about 10 years back who claimed he was an anti-apartheid campaigner who'd gone into exile.

He later went back, and took a couple of hotheads with him. Turned out he was working with the secret police, and those guys were lucky to get out of there alive. Not impressed."

"Me neither, professor. I have a low tolerance for deception. Thank you for giving me benefit of the doubt." He shares more detail of his reading of anti-apartheid literature, and they part on good terms.

Things move fast from there. Jimmy finds himself sitting with some physics grad students and an SGI rep, translating details of machine architecture into programming principles. Every now and then he has to ask the SGI technician about details not familiar to him. Correspondence with Lukas continues sporadically, much of it cryptic. Jimmy is left wondering if Lukas is making progress or if he will have to spend the thousand years his older self spent on the physics.

Meanwhile he sees Dianne every day, and by the time his CSIR leave runs out, he has managed to get a recommendation from the physics people to the biologists, who consequently seem to be keen to see him again. Barnardus evidently sees little value in being in Santa Cruz without a smart student to cover for him and heads back at the same time. The flight back to South Africa is a lot less exciting than the trip out. This time Barnardus doesn't get bumped up to business class, and when he's done boring Jimmy, he falls asleep in an awkward lump and snores like a wounded tractor.

Back in the office, Jimmy is battling to stay awake, with the combination of jet lag and being unable to sleep on the plane. He finds a pile of mail waiting for him, including pay slips. He rifles through them, and tries to calculate how much money will be waiting in his bank account. The CSIR foreign travel allowance isn't geared for someone who is happy to live in student housing. He grins. *I could probably think of buying a house with this lot.* That reminds him of the loss of his parents, and the money he's put into long-term investments. He starts up his computer, blowing off some dust. There's a fair accumulation of email, including a nice long one from Dianne. He has a long-lost sensation reading it. *Can I be in love?* As he reads more, the thought changes to *Is she in love?*

He has a huge grin on his face when Dr Smit walks in. "What's up son? You look as if you're in love."

Jimmy's grin shrinks into a thin smile. "Dr Smit, funny you should say that. I met this great girl and it didn't quite get to that, but I realise from reading her email to me that we both miss each other."

"Aha, and have you made plans to do your doctorate over there?"

"As a matter of fact, I have."

"Tremendous. We'll miss you here. I hope you come back, but don't make promises you can't keep. Will you be applying after you finish your M?"

"Doctor, they actually don't require a masters, and I am looking at doing something in a completely new field of computational biology, so they don't care about my physics background."

"Computational biology? That sounds interesting but what background do you bring to that?"

"You remember the weather project? I used some of the lessons I learnt on that to show them how to program a big multiprocessor machine."

The next three months are a bit of a blur, while Jimmy finds out how to apply for a Santa Cruz PhD, takes a couple of GRE tests, and develops a lengthy email correspondence with Dianne – sometimes frustrated at how slow the net still is back in South Africa. Once he has his materials together, there's an interminable delay for the departmental application deadline, though having someone on site working for him speeds up the process from there on. Early in January, Dianne emails him: he's accepted and she asks coyly if he'd like help packing, and whether he could fit a bit of time into showing her his home town, the one with the nice mountain walks.

Lukas meanwhile claims he is going great guns, and Jimmy accumulates a pile of papers Lukas passes him to read. When he gets time.

Nooby is after many delays getting his act together to leave for his postdoc, a two-year contract, and corners Jimmy, for once in the flat at the same time as his roommate. "Hey, lad, do you want this physics project to keep going or don't you?"

"What do you mean? Of course I do."

"Seems you are getting side-tracked into biology. Lukas is pretty sharp but he needs someone to keep him motivated, and that really means you. And keeping him out of his, uh, distractions... Girlfriend helps a tad, but she's not into physics, apparently. Maybe why I never get to meet her."

"Right, the chemicals. Here's a plan. I have some cash saved up. Inheritance, plus unspent S & T from my overseas trip. How about I buy a bit of land in an isolated spot, set him up with an Internet connection, and keep talking to him? If girlfriend is happy to go, he'll have everything he needs to keep him out of mischief."

"Maybe. What will pay the bills?"

"I'll keep some of the money back and play the markets."

"And always come out ahead? And how do you know the Internet will be a good way of keeping in touch in a remote place? It seems kind of dodgy even in bigger centres."

"You're forgetting my future self. I have some hints. And anyway the way we connect to the net now in this country is not mainstream: we're using hobbyist tricks because we're locked out by anti-apartheid attitudes. That will change fast."

Nooby rolls his eyes. "If the future self thing is not for real, we might as well find out sooner rather than later. OK, so where then? I've taken a few trips through the Karoo on my way to Cape Town, and land there is crazy cheap. You could buy a whole farm for less than a suburban house. And we'd be pretty isolated. No distractions, no one to suss out we're up to something."

"A physicist or two living in the Karoo? Won't that seem odd?"

"Naah, all kinds of oddballs buy up land out there. Some little towns on the N1 like Hanover are almost exclusively populated by drop-out expats running B&Bs and pointless businesses. Lukas would fit right in. And so would we, if we move out there after we're done with postdocs and PhDs. If you can fund us all." Nooby grins.

They track down Lukas, and after some discussion, Jimmy finds a farm in the Karoo going for a surprisingly small sum, leaving a fair chunk of change to play the markets. And Jimmy realises he's about to make a big decision that puts a major chunk of his future self's projects out of his control.

Life has just become complicated.

And then it gets even more complicated.

Lukas shows up in a state. Jimmy can't talk to him and escapes to the CSIR. That evening, Lukas is comatose on the couch, but Nooby is wide awake. Jimmy stares at Lukas in mild consternation. "What happened?"

"Girlfriend dumped him. For some reason he doesn't want to stay with his roommate who 'gets him' any more – can't get anything else out of him. And no, it wasn't the move to the Karoo. Lukas didn't get as far as putting that to her."

Jimmy sits next to him. "I know this doesn't help you right now but I exactly understand what rejection feels like."

Lukas sits up abruptly. "*Do* you? Let's get this farm organized."

And that is the end of that. Lukas reverts to his previous type only with more physics and fewer narcotics, and Jimmy feels relieved to see him go when the farm deal is clinched. "Nooby, I hope he'll be OK on his own."

"Naah, he'll be fine. No drugs out there, only physics. He'll get over the girlfriend thing."

Jimmy has his doubts but decides he's not the one to offer advice about a problem he apparently has for 1,000 years.

10 Protection

THINGS ARE HUMMING ALONG. The CSIR people are resigned to Jimmy's departure, so no one hassles him. His Masters is a dead project but he still feels a compulsion to keep on working things out. He's entangled in quantum theory when there's a knock at the door. A familiar figure appears in the doorway, a figure from a past he hasn't quite forgotten.

"Kobus! What are you doing here?" He bounds to the door, takes Kobus by the hand and looks at his still placid but not quite untroubled eyes. "I often wondered if you made it back, but I didn't know how to get in touch." Embarrassed, he admits: "You were my best, no, only, buddy in the army and I didn't even bother to find out your surname."

Kobus laughs. "Man, you were such a nerd. I don't know how you survived. Damn lucky they didn't send you to the border. Anyway it's Mostert."

"Well, can I get you a coffee or something? I'm not doing any important work here, about to clear off to the States for a PhD."

"Man, I'm not surprised, hey. But a coffee will be good."

89

Jimmy leads the way to the cafeteria, and procures coffees.

"OK, now what happened on the border? How did you get out of there alive?"

"Man, we took a few casualties, but most of the okes who could handle themselves got out alive. Me, I'm worried more about how we are going to get out of the peace alive. And I don't know anyone better than you to ask for help."

"What do you mean?"

"Hell, you're the only person I talked to who had any clue it would go this way. Back then in basics, I thought you were a blerrie kommunis, now it turns out they are running the country and vokken De Klerk is in bed with them, along with all the blerrie generaals who told us the reds were one step past satan."

"Well, a lot of other people, including high-ups in this place, had a clue a long time ago. But listen: I know a few things they don't."

"Your commie buddies let you in on..."

"No, nothing like that. I have a way of... of looking into the future. Kind of hard to explain, and even people with a good science background wouldn't believe it." He's thinking fast. No one would believe Kobus if he came out with this. And maybe there'll be a time when I need protection.

Kobus is staring at him intently.

"Look, you don't have to believe me now, but there will be a time when I have a seriously large amount of money because I know stuff in advance about stock markets and such. That's not what worries me though. Some people might get majorly upset about some plans I have to make the world a better place."

Kobus shakes his head. "That sounds pretty rough and I don't know how you'll handle that. Me, I'm just trying to survive this new South Africa."

Jimmy grins. "Forget my problems for now. This is long term stuff, not this year, maybe not in ten years. What you need to do is talk to MK, and offer to help out with security ahead of the elections. Nothing dodgy or illegal, just to get in with the right guys."

"MK?"

"The ANC's military wing. They will be calling the shots and will want to be in charge but they may be flattered by someone with real military experience genuinely coming over to their side and offering to help. They will hold you up as an example of the good boer. And anyway, the guys at the top are doing it. The ANC will eventually take over the National Party."

"Now you are kidding me. Are you sure De Klerk doesn't have some secret plan to skip the country with our gold reserves?"

"No, no way. They are going to get taken over totally by the ANC. They will totter along for an election or two losing support to Leon's bunch, then throw in the towel and join the ANC. Who by that time have pretty much sold out their own side too. Revolutionaries, it turns out, like the high life."

"Are you sure?" Kobus favours Jimmy with a penetrating gaze.

Jimmy is unperturbed. "If I have this right will you trust me on the other crap?"

"For sure."

"Then if I need protection some time in the future, can I trust you? A real professional operation, no laws broken, just make sure any important assets are looked after?"

Kobus is staring at him again.

Jimmy adds: "Of course you will be well paid, and if you can accumulate people you trust in the meantime, I can hire you all as a team, when the time comes."

Kobus shakes his head. "Man, either this is for real and there are exiting times ahead, or one of us is completely crazy." He stands up slowly, his coffee untouched. Jimmy stands up too. They shake hands.

He leaves, and Jimmy wonders which one Kobus thinks is crazy, then shakes his head to clear it. There can be only one answer.

11   Team

H E'S AT THE AIRPORT AGAIN, as excited as the first time he stayed up to open his Christmas presents at dawn. Dianne appears through the morass of jet-lagged travellers, and almost knocks him over. They kiss as if no one is watching, and the crowd flows around them. He grabs her suitcase. "Come on, let's get you home and into the shower, if you feel anything like I did after my trip home."

In the car, he's about to start the engine, but turns to her. "Listen, I'm not very good at this, so I hope this isn't a stupid question."

"Yes?"

"Do you think there's any chance we're in love?"

"Idiot." She answers with a long hot kiss. "Does it feel like a stupid question now?"

He grins, remembering the moment when he arrived back in his office.

The time passes pretty fast. News in South Africa is breaking almost on a daily basis, lurching from exciting change to unnerving violence. By the time they head out for California, things are not quite resolved but Jimmy is confident. "The spoilers are mostly bit players. There are hardliners in the government security forces, but they know they can't win."

"I hope so. I'd like to go back with you when it's all worked out." They are on a plane taking off from Jan Smuts Airport. As with Jimmy's first international flight, they have a row to themselves. When the seat belt signs go off, they put the armrests up, and have a good snuggle.

"Much better than my last flight with Barnardus,"

She gives him a look. "You didn't snuggle up with that old fart did you?"

His PhD starts out pretty tough, with a lot of biology to catch up with. Amidst all this, he and Dianne watch South Africa's first democratic election on TV with friends, marvelling at the long orderly queues. His own vote, at the South African consulate in LA, is nothing by comparison.

"Don't you wish you were there?" asks Brendan, a fellow Biology PhD student.

"Yes, definitely. We'll be back." Jimmy grins at Dianne.

Brendan looks at them both. "Are you guys getting married over there or here?"

"I didn't know we were. Are we?"

"Obviously," says Dianne.

"Oh. I thought *I* was supposed to ask. Are *you* going to get down on your knee?" Their friends find this pretty funny. "Well, OK, I accept. I don't have much family left in South Africa, and we've missed the event of the century, so I don't mind if you choose the place, as long as you go back there with me some time soon."

Their friends break out in applause, and someone finds a

bottle of champagne.

Somewhere, at the back of his mind, is a fugitive thought about Mel. *Older self, thanks. Thank you very much. If I ever hear from you again, I don't know if I can thank you enough. And Mel? I just hope all is good with her. But we have a new team now.*

After a very late night and everyone else has gone home, he pulls her close. "Listen, I have a little money in South Africa, inherited from parents, savings and so on. Not much in US dollar terms, but I have some friends over there working on a crazy physics project that just may pay off with something big. I already set one of them up to work on it, and the other maybe will want to join him when he finishes his postdoc that he's doing here."

He pauses, and she looks puzzled "So do I mind if you keep on investing in it? Is that what you're asking?"

"Well, yes. I had committed to it anyway, and it's not something I deal with very directly, but these guys are good friends, and I have no other good use for this money. It's hard to take significant cash out of South Africa. It's very complicated physics, which I barely understand, but if they have this straight, it could totally revolutionise communication."

"OK, I don't think you are really giving me a choice here, but I'm good. It's really something from the past but things for the future, we work together, OK?"

He holds her tight. "Of course. We're a team."

He feels a twinge of guilt at not explaining more. *How do you tell someone something like this? With Kobus it was a spur of the moment thing. Think about it too much, and the whole thing really does sound crazy. Not now. Not when everything is so good. Let her discover I'm a nutter later.*

He holds her even tighter. Older self is a vague shadow of the past: possibly not real. *Could that all have been a psychotic incident? But then how would I have known so exactly how the ANC thing would pan out?* He goes back to the moment. *Later.*

12 In Business

GETTING MARRIED IS A BIG ENOUGH step. Working out what to do next is even bigger. Jimmy is kind of hazy on the plan, why older him thought he should be at Santa Cruz and not somewhere else. True, there's a flurry of activity there, and talk of a new project to build an online genome browser, which sounds promising, but much of the hot biotech action is in Silicon Valley, alongside Stanford and the computer startups. He is contemplating all this after the honeymoon, when they are back in their student apartment in Santa Cruz.

It's been a rushed break, with a plan to take a family trip with her parents to Yosemite in a few weeks. A real honeymoon will come later, when the PhDs are out of the way.

He suddenly realises Dianne is staring at him. He blinks. "What?"

She grins. "Glad you're alive. And on this planet. You were somewhere far away."

"Just thinking. When we graduate, what next? I'm interested in some of the big questions, like what causes ageing, how to cure cancer, and so on. But I'm not convinced you get very far with that stuff as an academic. Tenure pressures, getting the next paper out, winning grants."

"And you can make money answering questions like that?"

She tickles his toes, a good distractor usually, but it doesn't work this time. He feels a twinge of guilt at not talking about the Big Projects, but he still fears spoiling the magic, starting talking like a nutter. At least not until he's made enough progress for it all to make sense, and his older self has helped push things the right way. He shakes his head. "Obviously not, but if we can do stuff that brings in enough money not to have to work full time, we can fit in a few side interests – research projects a bit too open-ended to win grants."

"That means pretty much we need our own lab, otherwise we'd have to pay for lab time."

"Yes. Though that's not so big a deal with computing. At first, maybe, but there's this thing called Moore's Law that basically says you can get the same computing power for half the money every 18 months."

"Wow. If only wet labs worked like that. Listen, dad has run a fair number of his own businesses, and knows a little about venture capital. Maybe he can give us some hints."

"Good idea. Let's talk to him when we all go to Yosemite."

She digs him in the ribs. "And since you've been on a distant planet, let's see if you remember what my parents' names are."

"Uh, Stephen who likes to be called Steve and Madeleine

who likes to be called Maddy, and you call them dad and mom. How was that?"

"I don't remember telling you the last part."

"You didn't. But that's what you always call them. I'm guessing now: your personal pet names for them..."

"Idiot. That's what people always call their parents."

A few weeks later, they are on a plane to San Francisco, and Dianne's mother meets them at the airport. Dianne asks, "Where's dad? I thought he'd be taking time off work to be with us."

"He's stuck at home. Talking to some venture capital person and it couldn't wait. Jimmy, Steve is really keen to spend time with you, don't you worry." She looks smug, strangely not annoyed at this turn of events. Jimmy decides not to ask.

Dianne gives her a pout, which her mother pointedly ignores, and gives both of them welcome hugs. They find their way to the family car, a Lincoln, which to Jimmy looks like a wheeled barge, though it seems to move a bit like a car once it gets going. Dianne is sitting behind him, and says, putting a hand on Jimmy's shoulder, "Funny to be in dad's car without dad."

"I wasn't sure if you guys were bringing a lot of baggage, and this car has a bigger trunk than mine," Maddy explains.

The car floats through the industrial areas around the airport, then out towards Palo Alto. In about half an hour, they turn into a leafy street, and Jimmy sees the family home for the first time. A Lexus is parked in the driveway and a lesser member of the Cadillac family is in the garage. They park behind the Cadillac, which Jimmy presumes from the casual way she parks it in is Maddy's car.

As they arrive in the house, Dianne's dad appears to be wrapping up a discussion. "Ah, kids, you are just in time. Geoff is one of my VC contacts in the valley, and he's really interested in biotech startups. I've more or less convinced him to help you guys with a business case once he understands what you can sell."

Jimmy looks at Dianne. "Did you...?"

"Well, I did vaguely hint to dad that we wanted a bit of independence and that you are a hotshot computer guy who actually knows some biology."

Jimmy shakes his head. *Am I permanently destined to be managed by someone else? At least I'm in love with Dianne. I'm not so sure what I feel about older me.* "OK, things are moving fast. Geoff, let's start with the basics. What exactly *is* a business plan?"

They all laugh. Geoff shakes his hand. "Jimmy, you at least aren't scared of showing your ignorance. There's a lot of things to learn about running a startup, the first of which is not to take failure hard. I can take you through all the basics and help you with the right kinds of things to say, but you need to be very clear on what value you are offering. You may have the most brilliant idea, but if no one values it, nada." He splays his hands out flat. "More difficult: you have to convince of your ability to deliver it before it exists, otherwise it's worth nothing."

Dianne's dad chips in: "We're about to head off to Yosemite and a week of clear mountain air will probably help clear our heads. Let's just talk a little about what you guys can do, then we can get back and try to turn it into a business plan. In an excellent bit of anticipation, Geoff has brought you a sample business plan and some hints to work through. Geoff?"

Geoff hands over a fat envelope containing some reports. "Steve, that sounds like a plan. OK, some brainstorming. Tell me the top three things you can each do."

Jimmy says, "I can make a computer do things biologists wouldn't imagine are possible. I have big ideas and don't stop until I find solutions. Sorry, that's two. Dianne?"

"Good wet lab skills. There's no new technology I haven't mastered. I get the big picture, I don't get lost in details. And I can fly a light plane."

Jimmy grimaces. "Not fair. That's four."

Geoff slaps him on the back. "OK, between you, you have a good bunch of skills that not many others have. What you need now is a problem to apply them to, otherwise no moolah. Think about that. I'll talk to some contacts too, and we'll get together after Yosemite."

Yosemite has magnificent trails, including some not too arduous rock climbs. Despite a fair crowd on the valley floor, not that many people are on the trails. Dianne and Jimmy most times set off on their own, leaving her parents to take a more leisurely walk. The air is starting to cool off, but the winter chill hasn't set in yet. It's a magic time, and as they head home, Jimmy realises they haven't talked business. He turns to Dianne, next to him on the back seat, but she's way ahead of him. "Don't worry, Jimmy, I'm sure Geoff won't be waiting in the driveway. We can read his stuff tonight."

"And make up a business plan, including inventing what we are going to sell?"

Her dad glances over his shoulder. "That kind of thing takes time. I have a proposition for you, so you can work on it without pressure. I've been talking to mom about this, and we both would like to get to know Jimmy better and spend more time with the both of you. I can't bankroll you for serious stuff but if you really want to keep the costs down, you can live with us as long as you need to, and you could take over my den as an office until you have enough money to rent office space."

"Dad! Thank you so much. But let's talk to Geoff anyway for hints on how to get started, because we need to get cash flowing in as soon as possible. You don't mind do you Jimmy?"

He grins. Management so far is good. He likes his new job.

They get back in time for a light dinner and then bed, and wake up to sounds of Steve and Maddy making breakfast. After a slow start, Geoff shows up and grins as the plan unfolds. "Seems you don't need me right now but tell you what. If things are looking good for expansion and you need some capital, I'll be happy to help out then."

As Geoff leaves, Dianne's dad turns to Jimmy. "Son, Maddy and I play tennis every Saturday but since we were away for the weekend and missed our usual match, we thought you and Dianne may like to make up a mixed doubles pair and take us on this afternoon."

"Dad," the word slips out so easily he surprises himself, "I know nothing about tennis except the people who play on TV make weird noises, so you'll have to teach me the rules for that."

The mixed doubles game is fun though he is so out of his league that even Dianne's superior play can't rescue them, and they lose in straight sets.

That night, they are lying together in bed, in Dianne's old bedroom. She touches his nose with a finger tip. "I hope you and the folks get on. I was close to them until I finished high school, then I needed a bit of space. I guess I let that drag on too long. A bit of family time will do me good."

Jimmy snuggles closer. "Family time will suit me just fine. I'm already calling Steve and Maddy dad and mom without thinking about it. Kind of makes me wonder why I didn't get on with my own parents."

And for six months, it goes pretty well. They steadily build up small contracts, until the cash flow is sufficient to pay for an office, then a small apartment. The work is hard, but there's a little spare time to talk about the fringes of Jimmy's projects. One evening, they're home from work before dark for a change. Even though the Big Idea business plan never materialises, a consultancy able to take on the hard stuff on demand turns out to be a win.

Soon after they move into their own apartment, they meet Geoff again. After working the numbers, he smiles. "You guys seem to have enough cash flow to do the basics without a big cash injection. I would be happy to put up a million dollars for a 10% stake, and that should be enough to cover all the growth you're looking for. Steve has a good lawyer who can check it all out to make sure it's all good and fair."

Jimmy says, "OK, let's do that, if Dianne is OK with it."

She nods. "Great, let's let dad's lawyer take care of the details, except one thing. What are we going to call ourselves?"

Jimmy says, "Anderson is a pretty good name, actually. The time to change that was when we got married."

"Idiot. I mean the company."

"Got you." A sly grin. "How about something like Intelligent Design?"

"Don't the creationists use that name sometimes?"

"Maybe. I like including something to do with intelligence even if others give the concept a bad name." *Like the military*, he thinks, but keeps it to himself. *They don't hate the military here like an old apartheid conscript.*

"We do genetics. Genetic Intelligence?"

"Too long. How about GenInTel?"

Dianne nods, and they look at Geoff. "I'll have to check if the name is taken, but I like it too."

After Geoff leaves, Jimmy cracks open a beer, and Dianne finds herself a glass of wine. As they settle into the couch, he says, "Ageing. I'm trying to remember what it is that stops cells dividing indefinitely."

"You want to do advanced stuff and you've forgotten the basics. When a chromosome replicates, there's a noncoding region at the end, a telomere. Each time this happens, a part of the telomere is lost. Cell division happens until you run out of telomere. We have Leonard Hayflick to thank for that discovery. Before his time we thought cells could divide indefinitely."

"OK, right, that's coming back to me now. But aren't there some cells that can divide more or less indefinitely?" He hides a twinge of guilt at not telling her about his future self. *Later, when the time is right.*

"Ah, so you haven't forgotten everything. There's some pretty good work going on about an enzyme called telomerase that appears to be present in some tissue types that do need more frequent replication. Pretty new stuff. There's a lot of work going on to characterise all the processes involved, and understand why unlimited cell growth, as in embryonic stem cells, is possible but not say in adult skin."

"So if I'm going to investigate ageing this is a good place for me to start?"

"Or even better, for me to start."

"I've a few other ideas I never got around to investigating. Is junk DNA really junk? Is epigenetics really a dead idea?"

"Tell you what. Leave the biology to me, and you focus on the SciFi." She gives him a playful nudge.

And so Dianne begins to build up a collection of ideas on how ageing is programmed into the body. Once again, Jimmy feels he is a spectator in a pursuit his older self took on single-handedly. *Am I abandoning my destiny to be a by-stander? Then again, I'm the only one on the team looking up stuff on epigenetics and junk DNA. And so far, I can see exactly why Dianne thinks it's all rubbish. But older me did tell me to look out for the good stuff a few years from now.*

13   The Nooby Machine

THE PHYSICS TEAM IS WELL ENSCONCED at the former farm in the Karoo.   Nooby has joined Lukas, and occasionally makes a trip to Cape Town to sell his services to one or two high-tech firms. And to tour the bars for the kind of company you can't find out in the middle of nowhere.

Jimmy takes Dianne to meet them, her second experience of South Africa. This is sort of a honeymoon as well, if not quite the real thing because some sort of work is involved. Jimmy promises Dianne something better will follow when things are more settled.   The work angle is something he hasn't explained too clearly. It involves complicated physics, and she settles for an arbitrary excuse to visit South Africa again. They land in Cape Town in July on a dreary rainy day. Jimmy finds his rented car, and they head for a small hotel in Franschhoek.

As they travel, he explains. "Franschhoek was started by French Huguenots, protestant refugees, who brought wine-making skills to the Cape.   It's a bit more rural than some of the wine-making places we went to near Cape Town last time, but they make pretty good wine out here. The name means something like French corner."

"I like the idea of a stop over in another wine-making region but right now all I want to do is sleep."

"That's why I booked us in for a couple of days, before we head out to the farm."

The hotel turns out to look rustic from the outside, but is well appointed inside, with attentive service. By the second day, it's starting to feel like home, if in a weird time zone. Says Dianne: "It's great to have seen a few wine farms, but I suppose you have work to do. Mystery physics project."

"Right. We should visit again some time when things are less hectic."

"What exactly did you say your friend Nooby is working on?"

"Advanced comms. It's state of the art physics, and he and Lukas have some great ideas that could totally revolutionise communications." He feels a twinge of guilt. *Lying isn't me. Must find a way to talk about this.*

"Sounds good. Me, I know biology and a good wine. Let's go meet your buddies."

They pass through mountains and some scenic country-side, which slowly morphs into featureless land with the occasional rock or sheep to break the monotony. Dianne is snoozing by the time night falls, and Jimmy is trying to find the right turning. She jolts awake as they hit a rough track.

"I hope this is right," he grins.

"You bet. Why this isolated spot anyway?"

"Nooby's idea. He said if we bought an old farm in the Karoo, it would cost next to nothing. And he was right. He put in a solar array with a big bank of batteries, making it independent of the grid, so he can draw massive power if he has to without anyone knowing."

"Why so top secret?"

His heart skips a beat. It still doesn't feel it's the moment. *Voices in my head?* He still isn't sure if telling her would result in a quickie divorce. "Don't want the competition to get wind of the idea. We don't have the kind of deep pockets you need to fend off corporate sharks." Another twinge of guilt.

It's pretty dark by the time they see farm lights in the distance, and a building slowly heaves into view. There are dark shadows above it, and shadowy forms that could be rainwater tanks flanked by a large garage disjoint from the house – with a battered old Golf parked outside.

Jimmy points at the Golf. "Looks like Nooby's car."

"Hmph. Doesn't look distinctive to me. But obviously worth less than whatever's in the garage."

They stop at the building and more lights go on, a figure silhouetted in the now open back door. Jimmy indicates in the rough direction of the house. "That's Nooby." And a while later, a second figure steps from the shadows. "And Lukas."

They get out of the car and Jimmy makes introductions. As Dianne shakes Nooby's hand, she says, "Good to meet you properly. Jimmy always seemed to be coy about involving me in your discussions. Or maybe it was just my physics phobia."

Someone else appears from the house. Nooby calls her over. "Hey, Esmerelda, meet Jimmy and Dianne." She's a dull blonde, strongly built and looks skittish at the sight of the newcomers. Intelligent eyes, if you can get a fix on them.

She nervously shakes the visitors' hands. "Esmerelda was staying at a B&B in town when I went to buy supplies, and tagged along with me. Pretty handy about the house, not so interested in physics, and doesn't talk about her past. Doesn't get on with Lukas, I think. They don't talk."

Esmerelda gives Nooby a look and he reassures her. "Don't worry. Friends. Let's all go inside, it's getting bloody cold." Sure enough, the temperature is dropping very fast now the sun has set. They all hustle inside.

Lukas points at chairs while Nooby asks what drinks everyone is having. When Nooby disappears into the kitchen, Lukas takes over. "You'll never guess what we've been up to." Esmerelda sure enough makes a show of not paying attention.

"Physics, I guess.'

"Well, duh. Actual stuff. We've had some real breakthroughs in quantum signature alignment. We can match up two objects in totally different places and synchronise their behaviours."

Jimmy nods. "Dianne isn't big on physics. Basically that means you've got some comms ideas, I suppose. Maybe give me some bed time reading?"

Nooby returns with the drinks, and makes it his task to get Esmerelda to loosen up socially. She sips her drink intermittently, obviously something not quite right with her. Jimmy catches her giving Lukas a sidelong glance, and she rapidly looks away. Nooby meanwhile is paying her close attention – yet somehow misses this moment. The social tensions kill Lukas's attempts at talking physics, so he ends up going to bed early in a sulk. Dianne on the other hand is obviously fascinated by the interplay between Nooby, Lukas and Esmerelada, and can't stop talking about the weirdness of the three of them when she and Jimmy go to bed.

Sunrise is not particularly early and Jimmy wakes with it still dark. He thinks he hears someone trying to start a car, then a muffled sound of a door closing. Dianne is motionless and he gets up quietly so as not to wake her. He goes to the bathroom, tripping several times over unfamiliar objects, then tries to sleep again. By sunrise, he isn't feeling too rested, nor is Dianne, by the look of her – despite making a better job of sleeping. They find clothes and make their way to the kitchen, where there are sounds of activity. Loud activity.

"Goddam. That Esmerelda seemed like a real find. Now she's buggered off." Nooby is not looking pleased.

"What happened?" Dianne asks.

"I think she tried to start my car. Couldn't figure out the anti-theft hacks and gave up. Must have walked off."

"In the dark and cold, so far from anywhere?"

"Obviously. She seemed a lot of fun a couple of weeks ago, but I wonder if she's an illegal immigrant. Or a psychiatric case."

Jimmy nods. "Nooby, you could pick up girlfriends with amazing ease in the city. You need to be more selective out here where the pickings are thinner."

Lukas walks in and catches the last sentence. He laughs. "Nooby, my lad. More physics, less womanising. If we get this all right, we'll have plenty of time for that later." He seems just a little too casual.

Dianne looks puzzled, and Lukas fixes her with a sharp gaze and says, "Obviously there's a lot you need to learn." She looks even more puzzled. Lukas has a look of someone trying to suppress a reaction, but is carrying it off well enough to leave Jimmy mystified – and his closest friend Nooby as well. A silence ensues.

"But enough of that, let's make breakfast." Nooby forces cheerfulness, turns on a few more lights and starts finding ingredients in the fridge.

While Nooby and Lukas fill Jimmy in on the physics, Dianne lurks around the yard. She reports back when Jimmy takes a break. "I've seen big solar panels, and a shed loaded with electronics gear. This all looks like very serious stuff."

"It is. Lukas is the real genius, does all the original theory. Nooby fills in the gaps and makes stuff. He's made a machine he wants me to take home to calibrate some of the experiments from a distance."

"What's this Nooby machine look like?"

"Not too much: headphones that allow you to pick up some signals indicating how well the machine is working, and a thing that looks like a computer power supply with a small antenna. I'm not sure what to call it because they are being a bit mysterious about what it does so we'll stick with your name."

"Dianne?"

"No, silly. Nooby machine."

She gives him a kiss. "You can name something after me when you have something more impressive."

The rest of the stay in the Karoo is not too exciting. Jimmy is too far removed from the physics to get the thrill he used to feel discovering something new. Dianne soon runs out of things to do. Esmerelda meanwhile has disappeared for good, it seems.

After a week, Nooby takes Jimmy and Dianne for some shopping in the nearest town, Hanover, a fair distance away on the N1 back towards Cape Town, and stops by at a B&B. "Is this the one...?" asks Dianne.

"Esmerelda? Yes. Just want to check if they know anything." He walks in briskly, leaving Jimmy and Dianne outside.

By the look on his face when he returns, they don't.

After a short stay that increasingly feels like a long one, Jimmy and Dianne are heading back to a life of new discoveries in gene sequencing, a mix of interactions with academia and venture capital, working with other start ups and even occasionally making serious money.

Jimmy every now and then wonders where his future self is, and in the meantime tries to keep up with the growing field of climate science. He puts a few minutes into calibrating the Nooby machine as requested, then forgets about it. Life has become hectic.

It Rained

14 The Turning Point

LIFE WITH DIANNE, the PhD, becoming one of the very first experts in a new field and trying to commercialise this lead all merges into a dull shade of grey at the moment when the phone rings in his downtown Palo Alto apartment. It's Dianne's dad, his voice familiar from the months they lived together in the family home. "Hi, dad."

"Jimmy, I have some bad news." He sits down on the floor, barely able to hold the phone, as the distant voice goes on. "Plane crashed. Dianne didn't make it."

Then there's the funeral, and Dianne's dad appears with a lawyer. "Son, I don't know if you're ready to deal with this yet, but I'm an old hand at light planes, and that crash should not have happened. I'd like to introduce you to Will Bush, who's handled some of my tougher cases. He believes we should file suit against the manufacturer."

"You're right, dad. I'm not ready to deal with this. If you've got a good lawyer do whatever you think best. I don't care, it won't bring her back." He doesn't make eye contact with the lawyer, but senses him nodding in sympathy.

So much dull grey. Stuff happens, Jimmy isn't sure

what. There are court appearances he vaguely recalls and genuine grief is obviously a priceless currency because his bank account acquires an absurd balance. What happened to join the dots is a complete blur. All he knows is he is a total wreck. First losing Mel, now this. Then he feels the familiar sensation in his head. *You knew this would happen. How much are the lawyers going to squeeze out of the manufacturer? Is this your sleazy trick to make sure I get the money for your project?*

Wait a minute. I only knew you were having some sort of crisis. The sensation in Jimmy's head for the first time conveys emotion. **I had no idea. If I did, I would have warned you, had her not take the plane out.**

Can't you do that now?

Not for you. I can only look ahead by going to you and if I use that information to go back, it splits the timeline. For practical purposes, you can't look into your own future.

I thought this was my solution to the Mel problem.

I really hoped it was. But I have no experience of this part of your life.

What has Mel been doing these last few years?

Died in a car crash last year in my timeline.

What? Why didn't you tell me so I could stop it?

It's by no means certain. Getting you out of her life when I did could have changed things.

Only one way to find out. Jimmy still remembers Mel's parents' phone number. He punches in the South Africa international code, after pausing to think through what time it would be there. The phone rings four times, and it's Mel's mother, Samantha. As he introduces himself he can already hear in her voice that it's happened but he asks after Mel anyway. For the second time, he drops the phone from numbed fingers, stunned at his double loss as well as Samantha's fresh grief at losing her daughter and grandson. The shock erases the details, other than a vague sense that Brian survived.

You have no idea how sorry I am about this.   A thousand years missing Mel... When I started to work out the quantum entangling trick, found I could talk to myself a day in the past, yet I had no memory of the event, I really thought I could save another me from going through all that pain.

And let Mel die?

We went through this before. What could you tell her that wouldn't have her think you are crazy? And anyway the only way I can know about something like this is if you know about it and then I find out through you. I can't predict your future any more than I can predict my own.

So you think I'll just go on with the plan.

I don't know. I'll have to give you space to recover and think it through.

You are me, damn you. What would you do?

I only know what I've experienced. This is beyond my experience. I'll leave you alone. You remember what to do.

Yeah, buy Apple stock and save the world. And if I don't?

I could start again, another timeline, maybe back to that day it rained forever. But I want it to work out for you.

Aside from losing the love of my life twice over.

I did not want that. I must go. We'll talk again.

The presence has gone.

15 Lukas

B EING CEO, CIO, chief scientist and whatever other titles Jimmy's accumulated at GenInTel means nothing. The settlement from the plane crash is enough to change the viability of the light plane industry. Not in a good way. It makes his company one of the few in the Valley that never needed serious venture capital, and he buys Geoff out for $10-million. He's watching the stock market closely, focussed on Apple and whoever else does well out of them. He's starting to develop a cache of information on key Senators who have a long history of undermining science. He's in the game, even if he is on autopilot.

He sees Dianne's parents on and off: he gets on with them a lot better than he ever did with his own parents. Calling them mom and dad seems so natural. They obviously feel it as hard as he does, and the mutual support goes a little way towards easing the pain. He's not sure how much time has passed: pain makes it all a blur. Every now and then there's a weekend tennis game and he's useless as ever. He vaguely picks up an idea that he's being paired with potential partners for life not just tennis, but doesn't feel up to it, nice though

they all seem. The tennis weekends start to get more regular
but his playing drops off: he just goes to watch and be with
people.

Then Lukas appears in the doorway. Appears. In. The.
Doorway. There is a vague pop, almost like the sensation
when the older Jimmy appears in his head, but more audible
than visual. Then Lukas steps forward, another strange non-
sound pop and Nooby is there.

"Hey, Jimmy, whose funeral you just been to?" Nooby is
as extroverted as ever, Lukas still reticent.

"My own, damn you. Didn't you hear about Dianne?"

Nooby looks puzzled then remembers. "Oh yeah, your
wife. What happened exactly?"

"Died in a plane crash. Her dad's hotshot lawyers scored
a huge settlement. Haven't you noticed I got rich and
miserable? Obviously not." His mood lifts slightly. "Sorry,
maybe you didn't know how hard this hit me. Not like I've
talked to you about it. It's been a pretty rough time. And
what's with the materialising act?"

Lukas grins, possibly the first time those muscles have
been exercised. "Like, man, we thought you'd be way ahead
on your living forever project what with us on the quantum
entangling case, so we thought we'd drop in and show our
work, and check out yours."

"Lukas, you weren't paying attention. Older me only
started working on the quantum entangling thing years after
working out how to live for a thousand years, and that didn't
happen instantly. Even with Dianne's expert help, I am far
from a solution. But anyway, do tell." He sinks into his chair,
the churning pain of loss slightly in the background.

Lukas for once looks lively, his presence filling the room rather than sucking air from it. "Quantum entanglement is about different parts of a system being linked somehow. Your future self found a way of doing that across time. Very clever."

"Or lucky." Jimmy doesn't feel at all clever.

"But anyway that got me thinking about space and time and suddenly it all clicked."

Nooby joins in. "He is so modest. It took me a week to catch up once he got it."

"You were only a few seconds behind him as I saw it."

Nooby grins. "Idiot. We've been working out the details for months. The few seconds delay was so Lukas would be the one who surprised the crap out of you."

"So what have you got? Teleportation?"

"Not exactly." Nooby strides forward to shake hands, Jimmy reaches out and has a weird sensation as if he's in two places at once, his vision shifting in and out of focus as he clutches empty air.

"What the hell?"

Lukas grins, his face *really* looking as if he's never used those muscles before. "The basic theory of quantum entanglement allows one thing to be in two places at the same time, until something forces them to be in exactly one place. What we've done is set up a rapidly shifting entanglement that creates the perception of being in two places at once, and we adjust the weighting of how much is in each place so your sense of where you are shifts."

"So how do you look to me as if you are here?"

Nooby chips in. "We aren't shifting our perception as

much as we're shifting yours. It's mostly in your head, nothing visible to anyone not connected to the effect. If there was anyone else in the room, they would think you were completely barmy."

"Not sure if I'm not. So let's get this straight: you are doing this across space whereas older me was doing it across time?"

"Pretty much," Lukas says. "I must say, if older you is really the same person as you, you're smarter than you look, even if it took you 1,000 years. We know what we are looking for, and it's still going to be a while to get all the details straight. Older you locks onto your signature because it's virtually identical, it seems, even if a lot of time has elapsed. The clever thing he did was to do that across time. We can lock onto a signature that's sort of similar to our own, another human, but we have to calibrate from close up. Once we lock on, space is no longer an issue. The time thing, like I say, older you took a while to work out and we aren't there yet."

Nooby looks at Jimmy, who says, "Now, wait a minute, you guys are doing things like looking at me when you talk. How does that work?"

Nooby shifts his gaze to Lukas, who says, "We know where you are in your perception. We have to project ourselves to you. From where we are, you are in the middle of a machine. We get a kind of weird sense of what you're perceiving, overlaid on ours. A kind of hazy image of what you're seeing and hearing overlaid on where we are. At least I do. Nooby?"

"Same here. Not sure how long I could take this. A few minutes, max."

Jimmy ponders. "So why can I see you and didn't ever see him?"

Lukas says, "Chances are we haven't found exactly the same effect as he discovered. You never gave us any detailed physics to work from."

"OK," says Nooby, "you picked up I wanted to say something to you. Have you heard from older you lately?"

"No. No, not since just after Dianne died. I blasted him for not warning me about that, then it turns out Mel died in a car crash a year or so back and no one told me, not even this bastard future me who knew it happened on his timeline."

"Well, that's pretty rough." Nooby looks as if he'd offer a hug if it was physically possible. "Why didn't he warn you of all this?"

Jimmy shakes his head as if to clear confusion. "He can't watch every instant of the timeline and didn't know about Dianne's crash, and wasn't sure if things would work out the same for Mel without me around. And anyway, I kind of agree with him that if I told Mel I was going to be in love with her and miserable for 1,000 years, she'd either think I was crazy or see it as some kind of bizarre emotional blackmail. I still don't quite see though, now I think of it, why he couldn't spy on me every 20 years because he would see at some point that I was alone again."

Lukas ponders. "If you are interfering in the timeline there may be limits on what you can see past your interference. The timeline may split many ways. I wouldn't be too surprised if he hasn't actually looked much past the times he's spoken to you. And if his main way of connecting is by synching with your head, he can't really look at later times without your being aware. If he talked to you any time after someone died, he would have to go back to before the event to correct it but that would create a new timeline. How do you know he didn't do that?"

"He said he didn't but if I never hear from him again, maybe he did. Maybe abandoned me as a dud and started a new timeline... Sorry, I'm not quite with it. I do believe he said something like what you said: you can't look into your own future because that would be a new timeline, and if he looks into my future then reports back, that amounts to the same thing."

Lukas nods. "I agree. I've done the math as you Americans say and I don't think looking into the future is possible. Not in any meaningful way, not so as you can use the information to change your own future."

"Anyway," says Nooby, "let's work with what we've got. Being able to talk across unlimited space and possibly time could be a useful tool for your other project. The climate thing."

Jimmy wakes up. "What do you mean, 'you Americans'?"

Lukas grins. "Where exactly is it you live?"

"That doesn't make me one. I still feel more at home in South Africa. Speaking of which, where are you guys exactly?"

"Still the old Karoo farm. Distance means nothing once we have the thing tuned. Kind of surprising actually how well this is working. It took us several tries to calibrate on each other so it felt like we were in the same room like this."

"Nooby, I remember older me talking about the power

draw he needed. This was in a world with meagre energy though. How big is it now? Not a problem for our solar power?"

"Right now, we are using about 60 kilowatt hours, not that much more than an energy-inefficient home. We can probably drop it a fair amount with a bit of work. What it would take to talk to someone 1,000 years ago is anyone's guess until we get the theory straight, but this sort of power is a lot if you don't have good technology.

"And it helped big time that we could calibrate using your head's quantum signature. No idea how we'd start without that," Nooby adds.

"Oh, the Nooby machine. I forgot that."

"The what?" says Lukas, annoyed.

Jimmy explains how he and Dianne named the device on their visit to the farm.

Nooby laughs. "He's right. You do the theory, I do the machines."

"Yeah, so back to my big projects." Jimmy changes tack to avoid a tiff. "Great we have this for when we need something more secure than conventional communication. Speaking of secure, there's an old buddy I had in the army that I should talk to. We may be into a phase of needing security. I think you guys will get on with him. He was pretty good to me when others were giving me a hard time. Strong silent type. Thought I was a *vokken kommunis* but didn't hold it against me, and visited me afterwards at the CSIR because I was the only one who seemed to have a clue about what was going on, De Klerk selling out to the ANC and all that, as he saw it."

Nooby looks at Lukas. "Well, send him over for us to suss out. Us guys are good at partying, physics, gadgets and so on. The army didn't like us, and we returned the complement."

Jimmy nods. "And Lukas. . . "

"Yes?"

"I hope you're off the heavy stuff. I'm still pretty far off getting a handle on long life, so don't trash yourself."

"Oh yeah, don't forget about that project. I could easily. Believe me, there's no better high than getting this physics right."

They disappear as suddenly as they appeared, with a pop that Jimmy is now sure is only in his head. He wonders when he'll hear from older him. *I have a few things to tell him, not only disasters for a change.*

Don't know if I can tell mom and dad this one. Certainly not if I didn't tell Dianne. He shakes his head to clear it.

So Lukas does turn out to signify.

16   Jimmy's Head

L UKAS BLINKS. He shakes his head to clear it and turns to Nooby. "Man, that was weird. I still can't quite believe we pulled it off."

"I keep telling you, you're a genius."

"Well, false modesty aside, tuning it to get us both into his head at the same time was a pretty awesome trick, and you did a fair amount of that."

They high five. Then Nooby turns serious. "Now what are we going to do about our lovesick friend?"

"We can't bring either of his love interests back. And after what's happened to the other two I'm not sure I'd introduce him to my sister. If I had one."

"Yeah, well, I think we should bring him here and quiz him. This Mel of his sounds like a bit of a head case, and it's not clear he should be blaming himself for her."

"Head case? We aren't exactly middle of the road certifiable sane either." Lukas digs Nooby in the ribs with an elbow. "Why not just send him to a shrink? I'm used to applying logic to stuff and I find people with head problems a tad impervious to that."

"Because a shrink won't buy into his older self story. Probably have him locked away." Nooby wonders what experience Lukas has with head cases but doesn't ask.

"So go through that whole thing again?" Lukas grimaces at the tangle of wires leading into a big black box.

"Nope." Nooby reaches for the phone. "Maybe it was both of us in his head at once, but I need time away from that thing."

It takes very little cajoling to persuade Jimmy that he needs another break in the Karoo; the prospect of seeing the finished machine entices him more than the clear country air. But Jimmy adds another detail. "Guys, remember I mentioned this old army connection, Kobus. Kobus...Mostert I think. I want to track him down. He is someone we can trust, and we may need security now we have something to protect. Having him around to the farm when I'm there will be good, he can suss it out and I can introduce you all."

Nooby sounds unconvinced. "You did mention this guy, but now you seem unsure even of his name. How are you going to track him down?"

"Money. I have the best PA money can buy. She'll track him down no problem. And organize so he's there a couple of days after I arrive so we can talk when I'm not jet lagged."

So in a few days Nooby and Lukas meet Jimmy at Cape Town Airport, and they set off in Nooby's rusty Golf.

Jimmy pats a sagging trim panel on the door. "You know, I've been thinking. With all this new money, we can push the projects along a bit faster. I've found little bits of money to help out here before. I can pretty much afford to pay for any new gear you need now, and any costs for the farm."

Nooby gives him a brief glare then returns his attention to the road. "Hmph. I thought you were going to offer me some decent wheels."

Jimmy laughs humourlessly. "I'm not leading the high life. The settlement for losing Dianne didn't make it to the media, and I want to keep it that way. Travel economy, drive modest cars, no designer clothes. If I'm going to take on big corporate interests with the climate change thing, it wouldn't do for them to get advance warning of who I am and what I can do. If you really want a better car I can get you one, but nothing too flash."

Lukas says, "Nah, just pay the bills and keep buying us gear. We can all splash out when we've saved the world."

Nooby isn't so happy. "It's my bloody car."

Jimmy pats him on the back. "OK, let's compromise. Trade it for a year-old model."

As they clear the Western Cape Winelands, the discourse shifts from wine types to tourism, how scenic the Cape is, and anything but serious matters of physics, biology or Jimmy's head. Then the Karoo opens up, the N1 a river of grey through a landscape of nothing painted with fine brush strokes, and conversation dies. Jimmy has been here in the recent past. Any memories it invokes are painful.

After an extended silence, Nooby pipes up. "Tell us about Mel." He stares at the road, the need to control the car an excuse not to make eye contact.

At least it's not about Dianne. "What's to tell? She jerked me around, married a jerk and died."

"But you blame yourself for all this. Can't you see there's

a problem with her behaviour?"

"Why are we going into this?"

"Because you need to get on with your life, and not spend 1,000 years beating yourself up. She was entitled to make her own choices, and they aren't your fault."

"Or I could just give up on the long-life project."

"Come on, you are never going to do that. Not now that Lukas has licked the quantum entangling one for you. At least the hard part."

Lukas keeps quiet in the back. Jimmy turns to scrutinise him for support, then turns back to Nooby, after finding only an impassive black hole occupying the back seat. "So what are you trying to do?"

"I'm no shrink but I do know that talking this stuff through with someone nonjudgmental has to help. Especially since you don't obviously have any other signs of a mental health problem. Get it all in perspective. Now, we have a few hours in the car. No need to talk now. You're all jet lagged. But if you want to open up, it's up to you."

There's a silence, then Jimmy nods slowly. "There is something. Al. She kept talking about Al as some sort of ideal role model, sounded kind of like me but totally flawless, sensitive, caring."

"Ah, a past crush?"

"I asked her once. She denied all. Just a guy who meant a lot to her."

"And she thought you were like him, and kept pushing you away. Maybe we're onto something. Do you know how to find him?"

"No. But her sister might know. Jenny. Jen, I think Mel

called her."

"Into the monosyllables. Mel. Jen. Al. You don't fit: Jim-my." Lukas is paying attention, it seems, after all.

Jimmy stares at Lukas in the back. "Damn you, don't trivialise this."

Nooby intervenes. "Jimmo boy, calm down. Lukas is a logical guy when he isn't high, which is most of the time these days. Let's stop talking about this for now, and see if we can track down Jen."

At the farm, Jimmy avoids the subject of Jen and Mel. Whenever Nooby tries to raise it, he changes the subject. On the third day, Jimmy is up early and runs into Lukas in the kitchen. Lukas pushes him into a chair. "Look, Jimmo-boy, we both know you don't want to talk about this stuff now. We've made a start. We've found the Al connection, and maybe Jen can help, maybe not. Just promise me this: when you're good and ready, get your real buddies here involved, and we'll help you work it all out."

"I suppose..."

"Don't suppose. Commit. Do that now and I'll get Nooby off your case, and we can talk physics and machines, and get on with our lives.'

"OK. You and Nooby are right. I need to talk about this stuff. I just don't feel quite ready. It's been too much. Losing Dianne when it was all work, work, work, and I hardly got to know her, then finding out about Mel. Anyway at least there's one upside. I have lots of money now. Doesn't replace Dianne or Mel, but we can work on the projects without having to grub for money."

Nooby walks in at that point, looking barely awake.

"Wassup?"

"You aren't obviously," says Jimmy.

They all laugh.

"Jimmo and I were talking about his head. How he needs to fix it and how we can help, but he isn't ready, so lay off, OK?"

It's heading towards lunch time when a plume of dust announces an arrival. Jimmy looks at it in some surprise and Nooby gives him a gentle nudge. "That would be your buddy, wouldn't it? Boere Rambo from the army or something."

"Oh yeah."

A mostly clean Land Cruiser parks neatly next to Nooby's car, and lurches visibly as each of two occupants emerge, one black, one white, the latter from the driver's side. Both are dressed in civvies but with the precision that comes from a military life.

"Let me guess," says Lukas. "The black dude is your army bud and the other one is his chauffeur."

Kobus smiles perfunctorily. "Hey Jimmy, it seems your buddies are just as good at controlling their mouth as you."

Jimmy shakes his hand. "Who's this?"

Kobus introduces his passenger. "This is Memela. Doesn't go by any other name. Old habit from the bush days he says. You remember you told me to hook up with MK? We did security for some of the less famous heroes up to the election, then they got government and anyone who was hated enough to need security got it on the state, and Memela was short of a job. Got to know him so I'd trust him at my back any day."

Memela strides forward. "And you would be infamous

Jimmy, the wunderkind who predicted liberation and the slide to the dark side." He speaks with an African accent, emphasising his enunciation, as if to show off his obvious education, an interesting contrast to Kobus's unassuming lack of sophistication.

Jimmy shakes his hand, remembering to do the liberation handshake: shake the usual way then turn your thumb to the ground and shake again. "You see it like that?"

"We fought in the bush so all our people could be free not so fat cats could skim off all the cream and leave the rest of us with nothing." He looked as if he could spit but was too cultured to do so. "I just about finished my degree in computer science when I got the hell in with all the insults and joined MK. We sat around in the bush for 5 years being fed propaganda and being given useless training. Then the Soviets collapsed and the ANC walked in proclaiming victory. The ANC has some brilliant minds, people I could really look up to, and look who they put in charge."

Lukas is eyeing him out closely. "So you don't think the change was a waste of time?"

"Don't get me wrong. I still hate the regime" (he pronounces it reh-jeem) "bitterly for what they did. My dad was a successful businessman and they forced him to sell his shop because of group areas. He lost almost everything, and it broke him, but not so much that he couldn't send his boy to university. I told him the day I was going across the border, and dreaded his reaction because he'd given everything to me and I was going before I finished the degree, but he was so proud. He died while I was away. I'm so glad he didn't see what our revolution turned into."

"Well," says Lukas, "the two of you seem to be good buddies. Imagine that 10 years ago, when you were trying to kill each other. So some things have changed for the better."

Memela grimaces. "There's that. We have great people in this country, except when we go to vote, then we are all idiots."

"OK, we need to talk business." Jimmy looks at Lukas and Nooby.

"Not us," says Nooby. "We have real work to do. Just tell us where we fit in." Lukas nods, and the two of them wander off talking physics.

"Here's the deal," says Jimmy. "We have some top secret comms stuff we are developing here. It changes the whole secure comms equation. Distance means nothing, and no one can detect you. There's more to it than that, and I'm only telling you because I trust Kobus. And I trust Kobus's judgment on who else to trust."

Kobus nods. "Heavy stuff. What's the point of making it if you have to keep it secret?"

"It's complicated. It didn't actually start out as that – a side project while we worked on a few other things. I have other big projects, like taking on climate change denial, and this could be a big weapon. We are talking saving the planet. There are huge disasters ahead if we don't stop the anti-science campaign."

Kobus looks at Memela. "See what I mean? Completely vokken bananas you'd think but he predicted the whole change – the ANC taking over, the Nats joining the ANC, the ANC going soft and corrupt. I wasn't so sure in 1994 when the Nats came second. But in 1999, when the DP cleaned the floor with them, I tell you, my spine went cold. And after Mandela retired, well, I don't have to tell you."

Memela nods grimly. "Look, I didn't study much physics, but I learnt about comms in MK, and got close enough to finishing a CS degree that I know my way around computers and networks. I can pretty much handle the standard stuff, counter-measures, sweeping for bugs and so on, with the work we've been doing together for private clients. But there is nothing out there that can't be broken if you have enough time and spend enough money."

Jimmy is impressed. "You're right. Nothing *out there*. What we have *here* is a totally new physics. Not RF comms, not Internet. Trust me on this. Your job will be to protect us against the conventional stuff. No one else has this, nothing close. I'm pretty sure of that."

Kobus asks, "How long term? I'd like to keep my other business going."

Jimmy nods. "I can understand that. I don't foresee *not* needing you any time soon, in fact more so as time goes on, but keep your existing operation going by all means. You could make up a cover like wanting to retire to the Karoo, too much stress, something like that, but keep your ownership if that makes you happy."

Kobus looks grim. "Do you have a backup plan? Some place to move quickly if things get hot?"

Jimmy looks thoughtful. "In the big financial crash of 2008, Greece goes broke. We could buy up an island or two. I don't think we'll have a big problem before then. Once we have an island you can go set up a bolt hole."

Memela and Kobus exchange glances. The word "crazy"

remains unsaid.

They talk terms. Kobus and Memela are willing to move to the farm and set up surveillance equipment, evacuation plans and unobtrusive defence measures. Says Kobus: "I have one or two other people I'd trust with my life. That's about the limit that we can claim are retiring to go farming without being too obvious."

"How hard will it be to persuade your other guys to join in?"

"For what you're paying, it's pretty easy work compared with what we normally do." Jimmy doesn't ask Kobus what they do.

As he watches the dust plume disappear, Lukas and Nooby reappear. "All done. You guys are going to have new roommates once they get organized. I would think weeks rather than months from what I know of Kobus."

Lukas and Nooby exchange slightly unhappy glances.

"Not to worry. They'll keep to themselves and they can handle some of the stuff you don't want to do like maintaining the buildings." He gives the flaking paint a wry glance.

Nooby shrugs. "You're paying us to do physics, not paint walls."

For the rest of the visit, Jimmy talks physics and electronics with his buddies, feeling pretty much out of his depth with most of the material. They also talk more detail of finances, but Nooby and Lukas turn out to have pretty modest needs. As Lukas puts it, "Living a thousand years will give us plenty of time for everything. No big rush for anything now."

"Except saving the planet," says Jimmy.

"Right," Nooby agrees. "But you can get professional

help with that now. PR and the like. And I might have an idea for you too."

"What?"

"Still not sure it'll work. Save it up as a surprise."

Jimmy gives him a look. "Well, OK. But remember who's paying. And whose head is being messed with by all this."

Nooby adds: "And who's buying me a new car."

"OK, right. I don't suppose there are many car dealers in Hanover. Should we go to Cape Town a day early and see what we can find?"

They leave the next day. Shopping for a car for Nooby turns out to be fun, ragging the used car dealers about details they neglect to mention, Lukas's surprisingly practical skills at checking out a machine making the dealers jittery. Eventually they find a late-model Golf that really has not been abused, and Jimmy organises payment. They spend the rest of the day walking around the water front, where most of the tourist spots are pretty empty though winter hasn't quite set in.

As Jimmy settles in for the long flight home, he feels a bit of a lift in his mood. The trip wasn't a total success, but he feels he can make it for now – and deal with the hard stuff in his own good time.

Forever

17   Jen's Story

NORTHERN CALIFORNIA CAN BE DULL AND GREY. It can also be brilliant and sunny. It's one of the brilliant sunny days when Jimmy feels he has done all the biology he can take for a while. The stocks are bubbling along nicely (not too much of a bubble he hopes), and he is at a bit of a dead end on the long-life project. He's set a bunch of PR experts onto the problem of countering anti-science spin, and it will be some time before they report back. At this stage they are talking to scientists and environmental groups, so he has nothing to contribute.

His thoughts start to turn to the past, and his not entirely successful trip to the farm. Mel may be gone, but he still feels the need to learn more. What *really* happened? Why did she keep pushing him away just when things started to look good? Were her parents still alive? Would they talk? Would they really *know*? It has to be Jen. The younger sister, always lurking in the background. They seemed close. He wonders if she's married. And who *was* the mysterious Al?

What the hell. I have money now. I can pay people to do stuff. Finding Kobus was painless enough. He calls his

PA into the office. "Maryanne, I have an old friend back in South Africa. Jenny Carter. Liked to call herself Jen. Had a sister Mel who died in a car crash a few years back. Not sure if she married or changed her name. When I last knew her she was at university, living with parents in Auckland Park, a suburb of Johannesburg. Could you track her down? I have her parents' phone number but I'm not sure if they are still around. I last spoke to her mother a year or two back."

"Well, this could be easy if South Africa has online white pages these days. How big a deal is this? Do I hire a detective agency if I can't find her?"

"No, no. Just do your best. You didn't need a detective agency to track down Kobus, and I doubt this will be harder. Her mother is called Samantha and her dad is Charles. Like I say, not sure if either is alive. Oh, and she has an uncle George who had a good Italian restaurant called Gregorio's in Braamfontein, another suburb of Johannesburg. He's a fair amount younger than her parents, so there's a good chance he's still around if they aren't, maybe even still running the restaurant. It was more his life than work. I think he's her dad's brother, so he'd also be a Carter, but try the restaurant name if that doesn't help." Jimmy spells the suburb name out for her. "And," he adds as she turns away, "don't forget to add 10 hours..."

"Of course. How many international calls have I handled for you? And anyway, it's 9 hours with daylight savings."

Thirty minutes later she returns. "Well, the restaurant turned out to be the best lead. It seems to have moved to a different suburb, but I found a Gregorio's run by a George, who has a niece called Jen."

"Fantastic. You're a star." He takes a piece of paper. "Still the same surname. Could be married even so, or divorced. Thanks."

That night he talks to the gang on the phone.

Nooby surprises Jimmy: he sounds worried. "Are you sure this is a good idea? You were pretty much over Mel when you married Dianne, and you just about melted down when we tried to take you there only a few months ago."

"Wait a minute. This was your idea, wasn't it? Of course I'm sure. I feel the need to clear the cobwebs, understand why older me was so obsessed with Mel, make sure I'm not going the same path. Not for a thousand years, for sure."

"So what's the plan?"

"I'll give Jen a call, see if she's willing to meet and if so, if you guys would be good enough to go to Joburg for company, we can all meet up there."

Lukas snorts. "I'm not exactly your ideal relationship advisor. But what the hell. I did offer."

Jimmy smiles at the memory of how he was the one with cold feet back on the farm, now that they aren't so keen. "You guys are friends. That counts a lot with the life I've had."

So they organise to meet up if Jen is cool with the plan, Jimmy feeling a lot less confident after he finishes talking. *This is it. No backing down.* With some trepidation, he makes the call. She answers on the third ring, her voice so familiar his heart misses a beat. The last time he remembers talking to her, she was calling Mel to the phone. Then a pause, and telling him, sorry, she's mistaken, Mel has gone out. A friendly chat ensued, and the next conversation with Mel went something like, "So you're looking for a younger version?"

The last time he remembers seeing Jen was at the wedding. Mel's wedding. A time that was a numb haze. *Why didn't I take older me's word for it and not experience the pain first hand?* He was in no state then to talk. He pushes all that aside. "Hi, is this Jen?"

"No one's called me that in years. Wait a minute! That's not Jimmy is it? Jimmy Anderson?"

"Wow. I didn't expect you to remember me."

"Of course I remember you. What have you been up to?"

"A long story. Good and bad. Now I'm alone in California with a huge amount of money, and just wanted to talk to someone familiar."

A long pause. "Familiar. Funny you should say that. It feels like we were talking yesterday but it must be, what ten years? Fifteen?"

"Yeah, something like that. Listen, I've been thinking of visiting South Africa for a while. Are you free, say, Friday?"

"You're visiting South Africa just to see me? Don't be silly."

He is, and does feel silly. "Of course not," he lies. "I have an office in Johannesburg and there's nothing like inspecting things in person."

He makes arrangements with her, and passes details on to Nooby. In a matter of days, he's on a plane. He walks through the first class and business cabins as if he absolutely doesn't belong, wondering how the occupants would feel knowing he could buy all of them out without a sweat.

He has splashed out on an extra seat to give himself some elbow room, and spends much of the flight exploring the entertainment system. Johannesburg airport leaves no impression as he finds his way to wherever car rentals are now, and from there to his hotel in Parktown, a rather nice place he remembers going to for drinks once in his student days. Then follows the lonely ritual for those who don't trust melatonin: keeping awake until late at night to switch to the time zone.

He wakes to sunlight streaming past his open curtains and a loud knocking at the door. It's Nooby, who's checked in next door overnight. They find Lukas at an outdoor table nursing a coffee. "Two days before you meet your girl. Can we talk some physics?"

"My girl?" Jimmy fixes Lukas with a glare.

"Whatever. Physics. We have the space thing pretty well sorted. Any ideas on the time dimension?"

"I haven't thought about this for years. Been scared to, watching you work. Didn't you notice I kept pretty quiet the last few discussions we had? I guess it's not really high priority for me. If we get the climate change things sorted, we won't have to ask someone else to fix their time line, and my head is sorted enough that I'm not sure I need to make a better me."

"Didn't that future you give you any hints? He doesn't seem to mind too much playing a little godling to his other selves." Lukas is sounding a little more judgmental than his usual self.

"I kind of scared him off I think with my anger at what happened to Mel and Dianne. He'll be back. Unless he gave up on me and started a new timeline." Jimmy stops and stares deliberately at Lukas. "Other *selves*? How often do you think he's done this?"

Lukas shrugs. "What would you do?"

Jimmy shakes his head. "Ask me in a thousand years. And anyway I've been focussed on the biology and climate politics projects."

"And how are those going?" Nooby it seems is also not in the mood for physics.

"Well, my angle on the climate thing is first of all to go hard early and point out the lack of credibility of the deniers, how they are a bunch of professional shills who did the same job for tobacco. Catch that early enough and get the public clued as to the conspiracy and they will get less traction. Also, I've been reading the science and it's all just physics, a lot of calculus, techniques for numerical simulation and so on. The average joe won't understand that. What they will get is fuel shortages and high prices. So I've been working on setting up groups to push the message of the dangers of dependence on fossil fuels. There's a bunch who talk about peak oil, and I've been pushing some good PR people their way. And finally, the real stuff: putting big money into clean energy."

"Wow. Busy lad. What's the key thing in clean energy?"

"Storage. There's plenty of solar energy out there, lots of wind, tide, and so on. But not always at the right place and right time. There've been a few battery ideas that turned out to be completely flakey, super capacitors that are showing promise, and the simplest of all, storing solar energy as heat."

Lukas looks miffed. "None of that sounds like cool physics."

Nooby grins. "Yeah, well nothing is as cool as what you're doing but someone here has to save the planet. Jimmy, tell us about the biology thing. If we have a thousand years we don't have to worry too much whose story gets told first."

"Not so great there. I've been looking at various angles. How cell death is programmed. The role of telomeres in limiting the number of times a cell can divide. The balance between a cancer's ability to grow indefinitely and the opposite case, limits to cell division. I have a lot of ideas but nothing concrete. I haven't in truth moved all that far since I lost Dianne. She was a brilliant biologist. I just followed along."

"OK *now* can we talk physics? At least one of us is brilliant at *that*," Lukas whines. Nooby tosses a seat cushion at him. But they talk physics until the shadows lengthen.

Jimmy checks his watch. "It's probably late enough to catch Jen at home. You know, I didn't think to ask what kind of work she does or if she's in any relationship. Better check now I suppose."

Jen is at home and not with anyone, and they set up a meeting for Friday 3pm in Melville. She has an ethnic art store, it turns out, and has someone who can run things for her if she sneaks out early for an old friend.

"Old friend?" Jimmy puts the phone down slowly, realising he's completely forgotten to ask about relationships.

Nooby grins. "You aren't that old, man."

"No, I mean, I've hardly talked to her. My longest conversations with her were when I was trying to find Mel. And that stopped abruptly when Mel wrongly saw her as a rival. She was just in the background in the Mel years. I didn't know she thought of me as a friend."

The next day, they drive around Johannesburg seeking out familiar spots. The area around Wits has changed a lot. Many of the good restaurants have disappeared, though the Nino's coffee shop is still there. The campus itself is heavily fenced off, and the hand rail on an overpass over the M1 outside the west side of campus has been sawn off by scrap metal thieves.

Melville is still its trendy self, though with a lot more high walls and fences than Jimmy remembers. They stop in the shopping district, and Jimmy takes them to the bookstore where he picked up his "subversive" material. Lukas grins when Jimmy uses the word. "Remember how *I* was the one who lost his security clearance. Meanwhile you all along were the real subversive."

Jimmy laughs. "That's because I'm so innocent. No one believes I can do anything bad."

"Can you?" Nooby asks with feigned seriousness.

Jimmy looks inscrutable. "Think of the naughtiest thing you've ever done and add one."

Lukas looks at Nooby, then at Jimmy. "Sex with three girls at once?"

Jimmy grins coyly. "Me? of course not."

Nooby looks at Lukas. "OK then, getting high on four different substances at once."

"Me? No way. I can never outclass you guys for naughty."

"Then why mention it?" Nooby gives him a you're deliberately wasting my time look.

"Just for a reaction."

Lukas laughs. "You are bloody naughty after all. Who'd have thought? Our tame little Jimmy winding us up like that. Let's get some lunch."

"Good idea. How about we buy take-aways and go to a park? It may be mid-winter, but it's not a bad day." Nooby thinks for a bit. "I know where. Emmarentia Lake. Always used to be a nice spot."

They find a small shopping centre the other side of Melville with a Woolworths food store, and buy some sliced bread and cheese. Emmarentia Lake is as nice a spot as Nooby described it.

The day passes slowly and despite doing his best to get into the time zone, Jimmy can't sleep that night and is feeling pretty shop-worn by the time they make it to their rendezvous at Service Station Café the next day, on the outskirts of Melville. It's a spacious place, not too busy for Friday afternoon tea, possibly why Jen chose it.

Nooby finds them a large table, and Jimmy hangs out nervously at the door. Then she arrives, looking amazingly like her older sister but somehow more confident, more sure of her own skin. She recognises Jimmy instantly, and gives him an affectionate hug. As they sit down, she looks at his companions. "What's this? Did you bring your bodyguards?"

"No, no. These are buddies of mine who are working together on a little physics project we've had going since I was at the CSIR."

"Wow. That's a long-term 'little' project."

"Right, we can talk about that some time, but I'm here to talk about you."

"And Mel." She looks him straight in the eye.

He nods. "It's been such a long time, but I can't shake the feeling that I must have done something stupid, something that put things on a wrong course. But she's gone. I was wondering if you knew anything..."

"Well, she was my sister and we were pretty close, so

maybe I do. But do you really want to know?"

Lukas pipes up. "We want him to bloody well move on and take an interest in the cool stuff we're all doing."

Jen looks from face to face and takes a deep breath. "OK. I hope what I know is the real story, and will help you somehow. When Mel was in high school she was a jerk magnet. And she was a sucker for the smooth talker. She had a succession of throw-away boyfriends. The kind you should throw away, but they end up throwing *you* away. I kept telling her she was better than that. Anyway, after she went to Wits, she met a super jerk called Geoff. All charm and no substance. When he visited here he was the perfect lad. Dad went out to light the fire for the braai and you couldn't see him for the smoke. But he treated Mel like a trophy. No regard for her feelings. Eventually she caught him at the pool with someone else when she went for a swim at an unusual time. Threw a dirty bucket of cold water over him."

Jimmy grins. "Great move. Wish I was there."

"Someone was. Al. Do you remember her talking about Al?"

"Do I ever. He was the greatest, the most sensitive, but she always denied he'd been a boyfriend. Just a very good friend."

"There's a lie for you. Al saw her delivering the bucket to Geoff, congratulated her on her aim or something, and they were totally conjoined. It was a beautiful thing to see them together. A total contrast to Geoff, got on well with me – treated me like his little sister, was wonderful with mum and not that bad with dad, just didn't do all the laddish stuff, like rushing out to light the fire. When dad did that, he stayed inside and helped with the salads."

"So what happened to him?"

"Another time Mel went to the pool at an unusual time. An old flame, of the pure jerk school, spotted her, ambushed her with a big juicy kiss just when Al, who also didn't usually go for a swim at that time, was walking past."

"And poured cold water over her?"

"Worse. Fled the scene and wouldn't talk to her."

"Didn't it occur to her that that was pretty extreme behaviour, I mean, she could have been auditioning for a play or something?" Lukas looks at his feet. "Sorry, but he did over-react. What did she do?"

"Pretty much blamed herself, was totally miserable. We dragged her off to the beach cottage for the Easter break, and she spent the first few days in bed crying. We had a beautiful place in Shelly Beach on the South Coast. Then mum persuaded her to go out to the beach, met a cute young lifie, David I think his name was. I accused her of cradle-snatching and she had him drive her to Margate for a night out to prove he wasn't that young. They went to some dive that plays barely live music, called the Palm Glove –"

"– Grove –" Jimmy corrects.

"– Grove." She gives him a look but goes on. "Anyway she gets back about midnight stinking like an ashtray, covered in beach sand, foot bleeding. David somehow finds his own way home and that's the last we see of him. We take her off to the hospital in Port Shepstone, where she gets cleaned up and a cranky radiographer gets hauled out of bed to take a pointless X-ray. That kind of killed Easter, so we gave up and went home before the crowd, thankfully missing the traffic nightmare we had on the way down.

"Then we get back home and she tells me about a conversation she overheard between dad and mum where dad says she needs to be managed by someone with a firm hand, not someone emotional like Al. She's clearly very broken up by that idea, then suddenly turns up with you and announces she's found another Al. Well, dad wasn't too happy with that though mum and I thought you were the greatest. Dad and mum kept worrying that she would end up an emotional wreck again, and she kept seeing Al in you and worrying that she'd done something to hurt you."

Jimmy looks grim. "Self-fulfilling prophecy. Seems no one was on my side."

She puts her hand on his. "If it means anything, I thought you were the pick of the bunch. When you were at Mel's wedding, you looked so miserable. I wish I could have cuddled you and made you feel better, but I had a stupid jerk boyfriend with me, and was stupid enough to care about hurting him." She looks wistful, as if thinking of lost opportunity.

Lukas prods Nooby. "Hey Nooby, we're supposed to be working on that little problem we almost had licked last night."

Nooby looks puzzled then gets it. "Oh, right. That one. Look guys, got to rush. Sciency stuff can't wait. Jen can take you back to the hotel, right? Jen, sorry, we got to take care of this before it slips away."

Jen watches them leave, quizzically. "What sciency problem was that? That project thing?"

"No actually, Lukas pretends he knows nothing about

relationships but I think he sensed we needed to be left alone. They're really great guys, the best friends ever. But I suppose also they need an excuse to do some exploring. Must be tired of living in the middle of nowhere."

"Middle of nowhere?"

"Karoo. We need isolation. Nothing to interfere with the physics."

"Ah, so that would be your Johannesburg office then?"

He reddens. "Well, it was a slight fib. I thought it would sound idiotic if I travelled so far without something else to do in Johannesburg."

She smiles at him, idiocy obviously not a total turn-off. "Let's order something, should we, so we don't put the place out of business occupying tables for free."

They each get a tea and share a slice of orange poppyseed cake.

"Wow, this is good. Great choice to invite us here. So tell me what happened after Mel was married. I tried to stay in touch but she wasn't interested." He thinks briefly of mentioning his older self, then thinks better of it.

"I wouldn't be so sure, though she wouldn't talk about it." Jen is a study of concentration, as she summarises years of weirdness. "You remind her of Al Komansky, a guy you've never met, so she'd rather be with anyone but you... How do you explain that to someone you care about? There were several jerk boyfriends after you, before she married Brian. Do you remember the lawyer?"

"Vaguely. She moved in with him, didn't she?"

"That's right. Treated her like a trophy girlfriend. I kept telling her she was better than that but she wouldn't listen, until he said something that made it all too obvious."

"What?"

"She wouldn't say. Just looked kind of stern when talking about him, then stopped talking about him altogether."

"How was her life, I mean was it so terrible with Brian? I tried to get her to talk about it and she never had anything positive to say. Yet she stuck with him so I often wondered if she had the misguided idea I would be jealous if she said it was all good. I didn't even know they had a child until I heard about the car crash from your mum."

"As far as I could tell he was something of an emotional dead zone. He seemed to be blind to her feelings. But she claimed she liked that, not having to worry about causing pain. Called her son Al, just Al, not short for something like Albert, and got on with her life. Never talked about you, the original Al, the previous jerk boyfriends. I mentioned you a couple of times but she changed the subject. Forcefully."

"And Brian? I was in such shock when your mum told me about the crash that I'm hazy on the details, but didn't he survive the crash? And what about your parents? I spoke to your mum soon after the crash but my PA couldn't track them down when I was planning this trip."

"Brian did make it out alive. Spent about 6 weeks in hospital. He was never that close to the rest of us. As far as I know, he got over it and is married with three kids. I wasn't really interested, not after Mel and Al weren't there anymore. Dad died pretty soon after the crash. Heart attack. He was in good health before. Something that hits you hard can do that. For all her faults, we all loved Mel dearly, and Al was a real joy. I still miss them both. Mum moved to a retirement place on the Natal coast. Village of Happiness. For her at any rate, it actually lives up to the name."

Jimmy is silent for a stretch, contemplating if he remembers a place with a name like that when he was in Margate, then touches her hand again. "What about you? The jerk boyfriend at the wedding...?"

"Oh, him. He didn't last. I'd seen too much of what Mel went through to put up with that. I was looking for the sensitive caring type, but they kept turning out gay." She pointedly looks at his hand on hers. "You obviously aren't, are you?"

"Don't think so. Listen, this may sound crazy, but California is beautiful this time of year, and I'd really like to share that with you. And who knows? You might like being with me even when the weather there stops being so great."

"Is this a proposal?"

"I don't know. What the hell. Yes. Spend a week with me, all expenses paid, and if you don't like it, no obligation. If you do, well, let's see how it goes. You can set up shop there, your stuff should sell well in California, if you want to transplant your business."

"And divorces are easy over there and you do have buckets of money so I can clean you out." At the look on his face, she says, "Got you!"

18   Back to Work

L IFE WITH JEN SEEMS SO NATURAL, it's hard to imagine how miserable he was before. Jimmy takes her to
meet Diane's parents, and they are genuinely happy
that he has someone new.   Then he's back in the office,
juggling conflicting demands of trying to make sense of
ageing and trying to make sense of the irrationality of the
burgeoning climate denial movement. The PR experts are no
help: it seems it's a lot easier to confuse the public than to
inform them. All he really has is some advice for scientists on
how to talk to the media. Jen meanwhile is exploring Silicon
Valley and not paying too much attention to his work, after a
visit to the office when she announced it didn't look like her
thing. She does however spend a good chunk of time nosing
around the Nooby machine and even dons the headset, while
Jimmy fiddles with the controls, to humour him.

The first week passes, then the next. Then another. And
Jen is still there. After six weeks, they wake up early, though
it's past the middle of summer and sunrise is steadily getting
later. After a long snuggle, she says, "Aren't you forgetting
something?"

He puzzles for a while. "Obviously. Some help please."

"First week."

"Oh, right. We were supposed to make a choice, and you haven't gone yet. Do you want to choose a date? We can go back to Johannesburg to be with family if you like. My own parents aren't around any more and the only people I have who are close to me really are Dianne's folks, and I'm sure they would be happy to make the trip to be with us."

"That first thing wasn't quite a proposal, was it?"

"Oh, sorry. I should get better at this with practice." He slips out of bed and gets down on one knee, a painful twinge of recollection at how it happened with Dianne. "My darling Jen, would you like to marry me, so we can be together forever, or however long my research allows us to extend our lives?"

"Yes of course – what the hell are you talking about?"

"OK, that's a yes, but there's a bunch of things I have to tell you about." A range of options flash past, from being hauled away in a straightjacket to Jen running away screaming the airport. *Not this time. She must know from the start. She's entitled to know what she's letting herself in for.*

He gives the quick summary of the visitation from the future, the planet saving project, the long life project and the physics project. *No half truths and evasions. If she thinks I belong in the funny farm, this is it.*

She stares at him in wonder. "I'm not totally sure if I can believe all this, but you really don't seem completely unhinged."

"How do you think I made so much money? Big settlement when Dianne died, but not that big. I knew exactly when to switch from backing Intel to backing Apple. How many other people were that lucky?"

"I'll have to think about this."

"Is that still a yes then?"

"Of course it is. I'll just have to work out whether to play along or take you to a shrink."

He grins. "Deal. Now let's see if Nooby and Lukas have worked out their side as promised." He types a text message on his phone, while she looks on bemused. It beeps a response. He nods and gives her a wicked grin.

Suddenly her eyes look strange, as if they are trying to focus inwards. "Nooby! How did you get here?"

Nooby must have said something but Jimmy is not in the conversation, and looks on impassively as she listens to whatever Nooby is saying. Then he says, "Shake Nooby's hand."

She looks at Jimmy in annoyance. "Nooby just said that. Have you gone deaf? And what's wrong with you, not complaining about him walking into our bedroom?" She wraps her sheet around her, climbs off the bed angrily and puts her hand into empty space. Her eyes go wide. "Either it's really true or I also need to see a shrink."

She shakes her head, the presence obviously gone.

Jimmy looks at her in some trepidation. "Really still a yes?"

"Obviously. I must have what you have, and we can't let it spread further. It's not genetic is it?"

Jimmy laughs. "Not unless we have a massive gonzo coincidence and Nooby and Lucas who as far as I know are related to neither of us nor themselves all have the same weird mutation."

The next three months are a flurry of chasing after biological experiments, seeing ever more useless PR specialists, talking to climate activists, trying to find useful angles on funding clean energy and keeping up with the physics crew. Meanwhile Jen finds a shop near home that's available for lease, and starts to find out what it takes to run a small business in California, along with long calls to family to organise a wedding.

Dianne's dad turns out to be really useful for helping with the business, and Jen finds herself calling him dad one time he's in the shop offering advice. Suddenly she's self conscious about this. The old man reassures her: "Don't worry, I'm happy Jimmy has found someone, and that you are comfortable enough around me to call me dad. I always felt Jimmy lost something through not being close to his parents, and I'm happy that Maddy and I could give him that."

She tells Jimmy when she gets home and he gives her a tight hug. "I maybe was a bit hard on my parents, but my dad wasn't the affectionate type, not a real role model."

She holds him close. "I don't care who, but someone taught you well. It just took finding someone to appreciate that, and you did that twice. Dianne must have been wonderful."

"She was. I still miss her. And Mel. Though not as much now I know what happened. You're what I have now, and that's what counts for us."

Somewhere in the midst of all this, they occasionally find time to talk about the various projects. One evening after a hectic day, Jen pulls Jimmy onto the couch. She puts a finger on his nose. "Jimmy, what do you think the older you was really trying to pull off? Get you to reconcile with Mel?"

"He intervened a bit late for that I think, though maybe he did have something like that in mind."

"What would you do in his place?"

"You mean if I have the means to go back and change things in a new timeline? I've talked to Nooby and Lukas about this a bit. I would still like to be sure that the planet saving project happened, but maybe connecting with a younger me before things went wrong with Mel would help. Maybe if I forced her to tell me what her problem was, or if I talked to you, I could fix it."

"Maybe. A simple thing would be to get her to acknowledge you aren't Al. I'm sorry I turn out to be second choice."

"You definitely are not but the way I was then, I couldn't look at anyone else."

She gives him a hard stare. "Do you know what emotional blackmail is?"

He looks uncomfortable. "I think so, what did I just do?"

"Not now. Your older self. Making someone guilty about not doing what you want. Imagine telling Mel about the misery she causes you in another timeline, however you go about that."

"I hardly spoke to her since she dumped me. I admit I was very hurt by what she did, but I really tried not to make it show."

"Right, then you find out how to live a thousand years and come back and tell her about it."

"That's not me. My older self in any case pushed me

away from talking to her, probably less than he talked to her himself. But, you're right, I can't fix this any other way without going into that. The more sensible thing would be to find her before she broke up with Al, and prevent that from happening. Then the younger me could hook up with you."

"Now you're making sense."

"That's assuming the younger you would be interested in a nerdy type like me."

"So what if I wouldn't be? You're pretty good as you are now, and maybe you would have been good for someone else if you weren't a total misery over Mel."

"OK, future interventions settled. I'll talk to Nooby and Lukas for more ideas, but we aren't going to try to fix up another past me with Mel. And I am really, really happy to have you. Definitely not second choice."

They are lying in bed again as it's heading into winter, in a dark early morning. She says, "Mum is so keen to organise everything. I would do it a different way, but why not let her have her day?"

"Why not? I don't care about the one day at all. We can do anything that pleases family. I already have what I want right here."

"You say the nicest things. I think. Whoops." She rushes to the bathroom.

He follows in a few minutes to find her throwing up. "If we have a girl, can we call her Mel?"

She looks at him uncomprehending. "Here I am sick as a dog and you are thinking up names. Oh. I'm an idiot."

They go together to the doctor, who confirms that she's pregnant. That makes everything all the more hectic. They push the wedding day earlier, a jet-lag-hazy event somewhere outside Johannesburg. Jen's mother insists on being with her at the birth, which involves the complications of organising a visa for her in a hurry, and finding things for her to do in between their busy work schedule and the birth. All of this is new to Jimmy, whose previous relationships stopped short of a child, and he's surprised to find that seeing the new baby has a profound effect on him. He finds himself wondering if Mel's husband, what was his name, Brian, had the same thing when her Al was born.

As he holds baby Mel in his arms, he thinks of asking Samantha what her role was in Mel's rejection of him, if any – and thinks better of it. She's lost a daughter, and that's a big thing to cope with. She stays on for six months, until her attentions become too much, despite the help she's giving with the baby, and they find a kind way of persuading her to go home.

19   Call me Al

TIME PASSES AND EVENTUALLY Jimmy feels up to confronting his final demon. With the steadying presence of young Mel, he feels he can put that piece of the past behind him. He has his PA do the now familiar thing of looking up the phone number of an Al Komansky of even more tenuous connection to Jimmy's past. Though Maryanne finds the number in a few minutes, Jimmy takes a few days to build up courage to use it.

The phone is picked up on the fourth ring.

"Hi, my name is Jimmy Anderson. Is this Al? Al Komansky?"

"Yes, this is Al." The voice on the other end sounds like *Do I know you?*

"Ah, I don't imagine you know who I am. Perhaps you remember someone called Mel, Mel Carter."

"Of course. Who could forget darling Mel? How's she doing?"

"Sorry to say she died some years ago in a car crash. Look, I'm in California now, but heading to South Africa in a few weeks. Could we get together to talk? Old times, nothing serious. I was close to Mel for a while but it didn't work out, and didn't really know too much about her past life. She talked about you a lot, but not much about who you were, and what you did. I'd like to fill a few gaps, put things in perspective."

There's a pause. "I don't know that I can be much help, but I'd be happy to talk. Let me know when you're in the area. Perhaps we can go for a coffee." He sounds distinctly reticent.

Jimmy drops the phone, a hollow feeling rippling through him. After all this time, with the mythical Al possibly at the centre of the problem between him and Mel, could it be that Mel wasn't a big deal to Al?

That night he shares all this with Jen. She gives him a hug. "It's been a long time. She and Al were only together a few weeks. It seemed at the time that he took it hard. Ridiculously hard. Who knows? He may have been through therapy and all kinds of other nightmares and put everything behind him. Anyway I certainly hope you've put all this behind you."

He smiles. "I hope so too. It was just a bit of a shock after all this time to find him so off-hand about the whole thing."

"Let's take a break together to go to see him. It's time Mel got used to travel, and we can break the trip in Cape Town, to catch up on some of your old haunts. And I'm also curious as to why he dumped big sis cold like that."

"OK. Nooby and Lukas need to go to Cape Town soon to pick up some equipment, and we could all meet up there, then fly to the big smoke together. Stay in a nice hotel. Nothing too flash – but nice." She has picked up that he isn't a big spender and nods.

The flight to Cape Town is as long as ever but with Jen there, the time passes reasonably pleasantly. At one point between movies, she snuggles affectionately, and he is reminded of a past flight to Santa Cruz. *Down boy*, he thinks. Jen snuggles closer. Baby Mel barely moves in her cot. They snooze for a while, and the rest of the time passes in stages of movies, computer games and light sleep, punctuated by meals at bizarre times.

Nooby meets them in Cape Town, and they head to a hotel on the water front. "Where's Lukas?" asks Jen.

"At the beach I think, but we'll see him tonight. His job is to make sure you guys don't sleep until late enough to get you into the time zone."

The rest of the day is a jet lag filler. Jimmy points out landmarks from his early years to Jen and Nooby as Nooby drives them around, though he isn't sure if he gets them all right. Even a slow place like Cape Town changes in a couple of decades. By sunset, they are back in the hotel and Jimmy and Jen are dead on their feet as Lukas saunters into the hotel lounge. What exactly he does to keep them awake Jimmy doesn't recall when he wakes up at about 6am with Jen still passed out. Cape Town in summer has glorious weather: seldom too hot, very little rain. Jimmy gets dressed and takes a walk outside, then returns to find Jen stirring. "I wish we had more time planned here. It's been so long. I used to resent this place because my family saw it as the only place worth holidaying in, so we never went away. But it really is a magic part of the country."

"Let's go out for a wake up coffee then, and look around a bit. We at least have the morning before the flight to

Johannesburg."

Another two hours in a plane and Jen, Jimmy, Nooby and Lukas are looking for their rental car in the bewilderingly different Johannesburg International Airport. Mel is looking around as only a young baby can, everything a new experience. Lukas tries to spot a helpful sign. "Man, this place is different every time I'm here and not in a good way. They keep replacing information with advertising. Can't you just buy the place with all the dough you're making?"

Jimmy laughs. "And then what would happen about being inconspicuous? I think I know which way to go. It's not that long since I've been here. And I pretty much found my car on autopilot that time."

They find their car, and then the real tricky bit starts: finding their way out of the maze of roads around the airport. Eventually they are at the same rather nice hotel in Parktown as they used for Jimmy's Jen expedition. Lukas and Nooby split off to unpack in their rooms. Jimmy picks up his phone and calls Al. "Is this Al?"

"Yes. This would be Jimmy again."

"Right. Are we still on for coffee tomorrow morning?"

"Yes. Not fancy but I rather like the Nino's branch in Braamfontein. The first of the chain, and not totally based on the formula."

"Oh, right, the one a few blocks from Wits."

"Exactly. See you there at ten? And maybe bring my partner?"

"Why not. I'll bring my wife and some friends. We'll make an occasion of it."

Jimmy ends the call. "Partner?"

Jen is in the bathroom and doesn't hear but as the group meets up in the bar downstairs to order coffees, he repeats the word.

"What?" Nooby grins. "Surely you don't think he's been celibate since Mel? You weren't either, were you?" He looks pointedly at Jen and baby Mel, sleeping in her pram.

"Idiot." Jimmy slaps him. But not too hard: it wouldn't do to be thrown out of the hotel.

Jen asks, "Did you mention me?"

"I should have. Silly. Anyway you used to get on well with him so it shouldn't be a problem."

The next morning they arrive a bit early at Nino's. It's a small restaurant, with tables outside as well as inside. Jimmy eyes out the layout. "You know, I think we should go inside because we can only set up tables in a narrow line outside." A waiter helps them shuffle tables together to seat six, with space on the side for baby Mel.

A few minutes past ten, someone walks in, blinking out the bright sunshine after taking his shades off. Jimmy stands up and walks towards the entrance. "Al?"

The newcomer strides in. "You would be Jimmy then." He shakes Jimmy's hand then turns to the door. "I'd like to introduce my partner, Kevin."

Jimmy takes Kevin's hand, a numb sensation working its way down his back. Kevin's handshake is as strong as Al's is limp. They all take their places at the table, Kevin's dominating physical presence diminished in the act of sitting. Jimmy manages to get his mouth to work. "Well, this is a bit of a surprise. You know, you and Mel...I thought you dumped her because of that ex of hers kissing her at the pool."

"My dear Mel. I was truly in love with her when that stupid thing happened. That big strong fellow holding her tight, administering that kiss and I just couldn't get out of my head the feeling that she was enjoying that so much, it couldn't be a bad thing. And then I imagined myself as receiving the same thing. It was all so confusing."

Al recognises Jen and prances around to her side of the table and they share a big hug. He picks up her left hand and examines a ring on her finger. "My dear boy, did you get married to Jen? What a nice surprise."

Jimmy is still trying to make sense of all this. "Jen told me about that scene and it did seem strange that you couldn't take Mel's word for it, an ambush, not something she wanted. Do you mean Mel made you go gay?"

Kevin shakes his head. "Nothing *makes* you go gay. It's something you're born with. Think about it logically. Without social inhibition, it's obvious that someone built the same way as you can give you a great physical experience. But sexual pleasure is not all physical experience. There's also a deep instinctive emotional attraction. If you're gay, that's wired differently. End of story. Al loved Mel for who she was, but that deep instinctive thing was missing. Right, Al?"

"I suppose. I didn't really think of it beyond that she'd be mortified if she understood why I really pushed her away. I was very confused in those days about who or what I was."

Lukas seizes a break in the flow. "We're here for coffees." He attracts a waiter and steaming cappuccinos arrive expeditiously, all this punctuating the conversation and allowing it to swing to small talk and generalities.

The trip back to the hotel is silent.

Back at the hotel, they all go to Jimmy and Jen's room. Jimmy and Jen flop on the bed, Lukas and Nooby into chairs. Mel junior is completely oblivious to all the fuss and sleeps through everything – as always.

Jen slowly shakes her head. "Well how about that. All that emotional angst over someone who walked out on her for a good reason. What a pity people couldn't be more open about that. Save you a thousand years of misery for a start." She touches Jimmy lightly on the shoulder. He isn't moving.

Lukas looks around. "So he turns out to be the biggest jerk. The ultimate chick magnet: sensitive, caring, athletic, sees the female perspective, then turns out to be gay."

Jen turns on him. "Totally not fair. I liked him a lot, and he must have gone through hell over this. How was he to know what was going through everyone else's heads? So: new plan?"

"Yes." Jimmy looks at his physics team. "Maybe a small revision in our ideas for tweaking other timelines is called for?"

20   Back to Life

J IMMY IS WORKING LATE. He sees long shadows outside
the office, and a slowing stream of late workers heading
home. He's about to call Jen to apologize when he feels
a sensation in his head he hasn't had in years.

Where the hell have you been?

Giving you space. To get over the anger.

*Well, that's been under control for a while.   Here's
something you didn't work out in a thousand years. Al turns
out to be gay. Got confused about his sexual orientation when
he saw Mel being kissed by a big strong guy, ran away until
he found his way out of the closet. Then she couldn't work out
why Al had pushed her away so hard, saw me/you as another
Al, and kept imagining she was causing the sort of hurt she
caused Al. Which had never really existed, but ended up really
existing for you/me.*

**You mean all this time I've been crazy about someone
who was crazy about someone else who couldn't be crazy
about her?**

Nice summary. But this is how I found all that out. He
shares thoughts about Jen, young Mel, the agonised decision

166

over the name for their son, eventually named Stu. Short, simple, no reminder of anything.

Just Stu, like just Mel? And just Al? Anyway. Jen. Such a surprise. I thought she was hardly interested in me. Sort of sympathetic I suppose, but she was never a major factor.

Didn't signify?

Where did I hear that before?

Lukas. Nooby. They do *signify. They've worked out how to use quantum entangling to communicate over space, if they can get a quantum signature to lock on to. Time will be a harder one.*

Do you think that's wise? Sharing the big secret?

Do you think any of this is wise? Look, I've more or less fixed up my head problems, and in only a few years. You could have spent your 1,000 years studying another subject constructively.

Psychology?

For sure.

Don't think I didn't think of that. But I had this drive to invent a way of getting back to a junior me to stop the whole mess developing and I wasn't sure I'd have that if I cured myself.

So you could apply a thousand years of emotional blackmail through me.

No! Didn't you back off from contact with Mel after you heard from me?

I suppose. Did you stay in touch a lot longer?

On and off. Every now and then I couldn't resist and called her. A few times she complained about Brian's insensitivity, then made it clear she belonged with him.

Weird, total contradiction of what she claimed she liked about me. Then I dropped it a couple of years and the next time we spoke, it was just like old times. So good. I could feel the old attraction was still there. I tried again the next week, and she brushed me off after the conversation started out OK with increasing impatience about getting ready to load up the car for a trip to the beach.

Ah.

Exactly. The car crash.

So you felt guilty that you pushed her into rushing the trip, that you could have caused a distraction in her driving. Happy now that she died anyway, without that?

Of course not. Look, I don't even know if it was her or Brian driving. I just know that less involvement from me could have changed her life a bit, made the timing different. They may even have not made that trip. Who knows?

Jimmy feels the weight of his older self's guilt lift just a bit. *Anyway that's out of our control now. Unless one of us creates a new timeline, tries again. The key thing is, being in love with someone who doesn't want that from you is an affliction. Punishing them for that only makes it worse. I've fixed that though I desperately wish I could have made Mel's life better, knowing what I know now. But there's work to do, work you are supposed to help with. And in the end, she was entitled to make her own choices. What Jen and I think of Brian makes no difference. Don't tell me if he and their Al survived the crash in your timeline. No need to go there.* Jimmy senses older him picking up his own recollections. There's a pause.

Right, how's the life project going?

Slow. I have a bunch of things lined up. Telomeres. Programmed cell death. Triggers for cancer – but nothing to tie it all together.

That's where changing your timeline is making things worse for you. I started out on a genome browser project at Santa Cruz before moving on to a job in a lab in the valley and was working on other random problems and stumbled on this by chance. You need to look at the way viral fragments are embedded in DNA. They represent a virus invasion that was successfully fought off but, in the process, the virus became incorporated into the DNA. That provides a way of adding new functionality in the DNA.

Right, so long life is a kind of disease.

Not exactly. You can craft a virus to modify part of the genome, and do it selectively. The trick is in crafting it to fix the problems of ageing, and there isn't just one problem, so you need a suite of viruses and a way of turning them on and off as needed.

Fine-tuning the immune system?

No, that's too hard on its own. You need to design a virus that binds to a chemical that stimulates expression of telomerase in selected cell types, then you can in effect take a drug that allows cell division to go way beyond the Hayflick limit. Switch it off by stopping the drug. That then becomes the basis for the whole therapy. Get that trick right, and you can fine-tune. There's a host of other mechanisms to work on once you have this one right. Add in new drug targets for turning on and off the various mechanisms of ageing, once you have the basic mechanism. The hard part of the trick is to design a minimal virus that only inserts into

the genome in exactly the right place and binds to the drug once there. You need to fine-tune its ability to replicate, and prime the immune system to stop it at the right point.

Neat. That gives me something to work on. Any more detail?

Hard to explain theory and abstract concepts like this, with no way of drawing pictures and connecting the boxes. Let me try a new trick. Dump it all at you at once, stream of consciousness, not thinking in words.

Jimmy feels a rush of information into his head. *I'm not sure if I can make sense of all that.*

Do you want some help with the physics project while we're about it?

I think Nooby and Lukas will need to brief me more on the physics before I can make sense of a brain dump like that. As it is I'll probably need to write this all down without a break.

What of Jen and the family? You said it's already quite late.

Jimmy realises he didn't actually mention the time. But looking into someone's head is not exactly conversation. Things leak out. *It won't be the first time. I'll let them know.*

And the other project? Climate change?

Slow. I'm up to here in PR experts and the only conclusion they can offer is it's a hell of a lot easier to confuse the public about science than to inform, and all the other side has to do is sow confusion. But I am making some progress in supporting clean energy projects. A lot to do there before there's a real impact.

And politics?

We managed to get Al Gore elected, but he isn't doing

half as much as we'd hoped. Trapped in the system. Kyoto was knocked back in the Senate.

Not too hopeless for you...?

That reminds me: Nooby thought he had something. I'd better ask him. It's been a while.

But first write down what you can of this. I thought of a few more things. I'll check in tomorrow to see if anything's not clear. The rush of information again, a little less intense this time.

OK, OK. But talk again soon. Can't you do the same with Lukas, pass on the quantum entangling stuff to him?

I would if I could but I have no idea how to tune to anyone else's head. It works for us because you're a slight variant on me.

Jimmy explains how they tune the Nooby machine to a person's head. *But I suppose we can do that because we have physical proximity to the head concerned. Once we have the settings, we can reach it from anywhere. We haven't worked out the anytime thing yet.*

There's a pause.

I don't know how you're taking all this. It's terribly hard to get closure on something that trashed your life when you don't know what happened or why.

Thanks.

For what?

For helping me get there in a bit less than a thousand years.

The connection pops out of his head, and he gets to work, only thinking of the outside world when he notices the sun setting. He takes a moment to let Jen know he'll be late. She doesn't sound disappointed so he gets back into it and doesn't notice the passage of time. When he gets home at 4am, she's sitting up in bed waiting for him with the light on. "Jimmy, this has to be a new record. I woke up to go to the bathroom about half an hour ago, and you weren't there. I was about to call the Highway Patrol."

"So sorry. I had a visitation from older me and he did a bit of a brain dump of tricks I needed for the long life project. I had to write it all down while it was fresh. And also we finally had a kind of reconciliation, us with each other, him with Mel. I told him what happened with Al."

"Oh, well, I suppose I can't compete with older you. This must be some new kind of narcissism. Are you going back to work today?"

Her face says no, you definitely are not.

He grins weakly. "Of course not. I think I have the main ideas straight but no way can I do anything useful now except sleep. And I want to wake up with family. Family from here and now."

21 All in California

THE LONG LIFE PROJECT finally looks like getting there. It will be years of hard work but the basic idea looks right. After yet another hard day at the lab, Jimmy feels the need to switch focus. So when Nooby calls he is in the mood for something new on the physics front.

"Hey Noobs."

"You didn't call me that before."

"Welcome to Planet Monosyllable. That didn't come out quite right. How about planet Mono?"

"Still two syllables. Planet Mon... Plan Mon. Why the frisky mood?"

"The life project is finally getting somewhere. Older me gave me some hints, flung some kind of brain dump trick at me. I didn't quite get *all* the details but it helped a lot."

"Interesting. Lukas and I've been trying out some ideas that could have some similarity to this. We've been sharing stuff with each other as an experiment though since we are pretty much up to date with each other, it's not a great test. Want some?"

"Later. My head's full. I've been meaning to ask. What

was the cool new idea you hinted at a few years back? Was it this? Been expecting to hear something by now. But got stuck on the life project."

"No, something else. That's what I want to talk about now. I think we finally have it right, and even with Lukas on the team, it took a while. Basic idea is a trick to get a quantum signature without having to stick someone's head in a machine."

"All right. So you can mysteriously appear in their presence and confuse the hell out of them."

"Exactimo. Listen: we still need to work the bugs out but the basic thing is, if we can pinpoint the geographic location where a person is, we can get a quantum signature out of their head. It's still a lot easier if you are physically close to the person but you could for example combine a surveillance camera with GPS information and provided the person wasn't in a crowded place, you could in principle have a point and click user interface to nab their signature, and set them up for future comms."

"All without them knowing?"

"Right."

"How does it work not having physical proximity?"

"The effect works anywhere in the universe. It's basically a property of the universe we're tweaking, so you don't have to be close to actually deploy the effect –'

"– as you demonstrated to me –"

"Right. You do however need to know which quantum signature you're locking onto and having a device you can physically point in the right direction is useful. That doesn't entirely make sense as I've explained it, but it's about three pages of equations to explain properly."

"Best we don't tell too many people about this. Not just the ones we might use it on. Imagine if a government got hold of this."

"Yeah, I hope this link is as secure as advertised."

Jimmy contemplates briefly. "Inconspicuous means the chances are that no one with the smarts to do serious code breaking will be listening. Your basic voice over IP encryption is not that hard to crack but if we use something fancier, it will only draw attention. Let's not chance it again though. In future, stuff we need to keep really secret goes via the Nooby machine."

"Or face to face."

"Is that a hint? Would you and Lukas maybe like to visit here for a bit? Getting bored with farm life?"

"Well, yes. And there are things we can probably find out by visiting a few physics profs and asking them questions. Using tricks like showing up at a seminar and asking interesting questions to get their attention. Hard to do from the other side of the world."

"OK, let's set it up. My PA can handle the detail."

"Your PA? You keep mentioning that. We do everything ourselves."

"Do you want one too?"

"Forget it. Just get us to the bright lights. I don't need an army of bureaucrats getting under foot. Lukas thinks, I do, you pay. That's all it takes to get stuff done."

Jimmy grins, but doesn't tell Nooby that a small, select office staff is nothing like the army of Vogons you usually find in a big organisation. He will see soon enough for himself.

A couple of weeks later, Jimmy meets Nooby and Lukas at the San Francisco airport. Nooby looks at him speculatively. "No PA? I thought you had an army to delegate stuff to."

Jimmy grins. "The point of delegating is to free up time for stuff you want to do. Like meet your friends at the airport. Same as we got ourselves an au pair so we could spend more time doing stuff we want, not picking up around the house. I don't throw money around, but why not spend a bit on little things that make a difference?"

"Whatever. How are you man? Long time no see."

"Great. Let's get your luggage and get on home. Jen is chasing kid problems, but she's keen to see you again too."

Back home, Jen is on the phone, talking urgently. "Yes, I know this is a common problem and everyone gets it. All I want to know is how soon..." She spots the new arrivals. "You guys all had chicken pox?"

Lukas shakes his head, and Nooby nods.

She turns back to the phone. "I got a visitor who hasn't had it. OK, anti-virals the instant he shows symptoms. Right." She ends the call. "Bloody GP. We pay extra for personal service but it's still a big deal to get him on the phone. Lukas, chicken pox late in life can be a right pain, but if you catch it and we treat it fast, you'll at least have some immunity in future, and the GP says anti-virals can stop it going too far. Or would you rather we check you into a hotel?"

Jimmy is annoyed. "Didn't you know this before we invited them?"

"That Stu had chicken pox? No. He had a fever a few days before you organised the trip, and the spots only started to show today. Mel's just had it and must have passed it on. Lukas, what do you want to do?"

"What the hell. I'll catch it and get over it."

She gives them both a brief hug. "Listen, I have to deal with a bunch of stuff that went on the back burner while I was trying to sort out what Stu was coming down with, and I now have to deal with Mel going crazy for lack of attention, like being late getting her lunch. This all has to happen when Jane's taken the day off. Why don't you guys take a shower and go out for lunch? I should have things under control by the time you get back."

Jimmy takes them into Palo Alto. "There's a little bistro I go to some times, St. Michael's Alley. Not too pretentious, we should be able to get a nice enough lunch to stave off jet lag."

As they walk from the car, Nooby is looking around.

Lukas gives him a stare. "What are you looking for now? Not enough babes in sticksville?"

Nooby smiles. "Got it in one."

Jimmy steers them into the restaurant. "Time enough later for that. You look asleep on your feet."

They find a table and start reading the menu. Nooby spots something. "On the same subject, I see they have savoury tart. Mmm." No one pays attention, so he changes direction. "Hey, Lukas, you never seem to have a love interest except the one time you don't want to talk about. What's the story?"

"Just the one. Thought she saw me as the love of her life, then suddenly she was gone. Along with a whole chunk of my life history. For reasons I *really* don't want to talk about right now."

"Ah," adds Nooby. "An unsavoury tart." When no one reacts, his face lightens up, as if trying yet another tack. Jimmy wonders what's next, and pointedly studies the menu. "OK, Lukas, maybe a sore point," Nooby says jocularly. "What was her name, then?"

Lukas looks at him levelly. "Esmerelda."

22   The Tickle Monster

JEN LOOKS UNCHARACTERISTICALLY SERIOUS as she's reading in bed. Jimmy peaks around the cover to see the title and reads out, "*Slow Death by Rubber Duck.* What's this? A horror story?"

"Might as well be. Just about everything made of plastic could be poisoning us and worse still, the kids. Toys that have a rubbery feel are made of a plastic that leaches out ugly chemicals."

"So we don't buy toys like that. Tell the au pair to screen anything she takes near the kids. Jane's a good kid. Even if she thinks we're crazy..."

"There's lots more: all kinds of chemicals used in agriculture and sold into suburban gardening. I'm an artsy person. I worry easily but I know my limits. I can't go and check on the science. You tell me: is this all for real? *Should* I worry?"

He pages through the book. "It will need some research but it makes sense as far as I can tell. Hormones do work at very low concentrations, and artificial compounds that mimic the effects of natural ones by binding in the same way are a hot part of drugs research." He pages through a bit more. "Hey, I like this bit. Young mothers with babies invade a politician's office. Turns around the logic of politicians winning easy points by kissing babies."

"I didn't get to that bit yet. *Will* you check on this stuff? I'm serious. If this stuff is poisoning our kids, I want to get it all out of our lives.

"OK, I will. Let's go to sleep now. I have to keep the guys awake tomorrow to get them into the time zone, and it's no good if I'm too tired to stay awake."

The next day, Lukas and Nooby are slow to wake up, and when they finally surface, Jimmy suggests they take a long walk to get into the time zone, while he researches deadly ducks and the like. "The streets here are all pretty regular. You can't get lost but just in case, take my cell phone. I set up 'home' in the address book."

Jimmy is so engrossed in tracking down evidence that he almost forgets lunch until he hears the au pair in the kitchen. "Hi Jane. Lucky you're here. I would have forgotten to feed the kids." Stu and Mel stare at him with puppy's eyes.

"OK, OK. When did I teach you so well about guilt? I promise I won't do it again if you don't do that again."

"No, dad!" says Mel. "You're supposed to do something nice like get us ice cream."

Jimmy laughs. "Daddy's doing really important work because he loves you and wants to look after you."

Mel looks serious. "Important enough to starve us to death?"

"Enough. Let's see what Jane's made for us." He looks at his watch. "And I'd better find out what the guys are up to. I thought I was going to entertain them today." He calls his cell number and Nooby answers on the first ring.

"Hey Jimmo, we've found some nice book stores, and had a few coffees."

"Great. I'm still working on the rubber duck thing. Do you guys need lunch?"

"Yes, but the coffee shops look good and walking is keeping us awake."

So Jimmy, Jane and the kids have lunch together, a change from the routine, while the visitors for whom he's made the change are still out.

Back in his study, he finishes the job in good time for Jen to see his handiwork, and prints off a long list of plastics to eliminate from the household. He's ready to spill all this but Jen isn't there. He lets the au pair out, then settles the kids in to watch some TV cartoons.

Nooby and Lukas amble in. "Hi guys. Want to catch some cartoons? This stuff is not as good as I remember, but maybe I wasn't so discerning when I was six." They all flop down on bean bags, and try to enjoy crude formulaic kiddy animations.

It is getting late and Jimmy is concerned that Jen isn't home. The kids are getting unruly, and it's unusual for her not to shut up shop and be home before 7pm. He turns to Nooby and Lukas. "Any of you up for looking after the kids if I go see what's happening at the shop? Jen should be home by now and isn't answering her phone."

Nooby shrugs but Lukas looks keen. "I used to be a kid, I think. I can do this."

The kids aren't so sure, and start clamouring for attention.

Lukas raises his arms into the air, pointing his fingers down in talon pose. "Watch out for the tickle monster!"

The fingers seek out armpits, and the kids are in fits of crazy giggles as Jimmy heads for the front door. As he gets there, he hears a car in the driveway. It's Jen. She rushes into the house.

"Oh my gosh, I'm so late, I was making a sale to this great customer and forgot the most important thing in my life. You must all be frantic. Oh."

She looks at the kids romping on the floor, with Lukas jumping up and down yelling, "Tickle monster".

"Looks like you are all in good hands."

The kids rush to her and say in unison: "Can we keep him?"

23   The Nooby Trick

THE TEAM SETTLES INTO a rhythm. Nooby and Lukas squirrel away in a back room behind the biology lab, with an increasing array of wires, electronic components and computers. Every week or so, they emerge and give Jimmy a few hints as to how they are progressing. The gap between a page of equations and making something work turns out to be frustratingly hard, but they are getting there. Though Nooby is the doer, he is not as practical as a career engineer or technician, and has to work through practicalities a few times before trying to build something – and still sometimes gets the details wrong.

Even so, at their first meeting, Nooby has to admit there are advantages to having a professional staff. "Jimmy, that PA of yours is amazing. She has no clue about the technologies we're working with, but she finds everything I need without a sweat. How did you organise that? I remember the university admin as bureaucrats whose sole skill was getting in the way of progress. And don't remind me of the army and the CSIR."

Jimmy grins. "You mean the Vogons? I remember them well and there's no way I would set myself up for that. So I thought it through before we started hiring. Simple. Have a very small staff, pay them well, and try people out on short contracts before making anything permanent. Maryanne is my fourth PA, and the only one to last more than a week. I give her an increase at least double inflation every year, and she only has to show me a job ad that looks like she could fill it that pays more, and I beat it. One person like that, paid about double the industry average, does more work than four paid the industry average."

Lukas is impressed for once. "Not so hotshot at physics, a whole lot of emotional train wrecks, but you do have a clue about something."

Jimmy looks at him for a while. "Thanks. I think."

Meanwhile the long life project is making steady strides, again subject to the limits of just one person turning the theory to reality. Jimmy is constantly reminded of how he misses Dianne's deft skill at biology lab work, and his attempts at palming off small parts of the project on his own lab team are necessarily limited by keeping the main aim of the project secret.

Stu's chicken pox passes, and nothing happens to Lukas, and the GP concludes he lucked out – either didn't get it despite the high risk of contagion or had it so mildly, he didn't notice. In the meantime, family life continues, with kids' parties – with careful attention to the plastics used for snack containers – and occasional absences of Jimmy from the office to help Jen run the shop.

Six weeks after Nooby and Lukas's arrival, Lukas walks triumphantly into Jimmy's office, carrying a box about half the size of a shoebox. "We're ready to test. All we need is a target."

Jimmy looks thoughtful. "I've been giving that some thought. Probably best first time around to work on someone we know, so we can talk to them about how it went.

"Is there any reason to try it out on someone we haven't previously calibrated for on the old machine?"

"Not really. If we were publishing a scientific paper, we would need to do that, and we will eventually target new people, but we can set up the machine with no previous settings and start from scratch."

"Well then, how about we try talking to Nooby on the other side of the building? How soon can we set that up?"

"Right now. I have the equipment with me." He holds up the box.

Jimmy peers inside. It appears to contain a cell phone, and a small keypad, attached to a crude box containing a mess of wires and electronics components, with a pair of double-A batteries on the bottom. "Is that all?"

"Pretty much. The phone has wireless internet, and we can use that to tap into GPS locations. There's a camera in our lab, and I've rigged this so that a webcam on a device with GPS can be used to get a rough fix on a target, and once you have that, you type the GPS location on the keypad, and from there, the machine locks on to the nearest brain quantum signature. A bit crude but getting the rest right is detail."

"And the big machine on the other side, the one the person invading the other head has to hook into?"

"No need for proximity. We can link to a quantum signature on that machine too now. It's all just information, no energy, once you have the big machine going."

"OK, so whose quantum signature is set up to talk?"

"Both of ours. Would you like to give it a try?"

"Why not? What do I do?"

"Hold on a minute, I'll set it up." Lukas pulls out the phone, and uses a web browser on its screen to apply some settings. Suddenly Jimmy *feels* Nooby, as if he's in the room, somewhere close to his desk, but can't see him. "Weird."

You're telling me. Jimmy? I didn't expect this.

You didn't? It's your machine.

Bloody Lukas. He said he was just going to show you the box, tell you we were ready to test.

Well, is it working?

Assuming you didn't cheat and use a stored up quantum signature, yes. Now stop. I'm in the middle of something. Let's talk about this tonight, what we're actually going to use it for.

Jimmy looks at Lukas quizzically. "Switch off?" Lukas asks. Jimmy nods, then, as the strange sensation in his head fizzes out, high fives Lukas, who is uncharacteristically fired up.

That evening, they pull chairs around in a circle. Jen walks in with Mel and Stu in tow as they sit down. "Can I join in? Or is this boy talk?"

Jimmy pulls up another chair. "Strategising. We can use another intelligent head here."

"Well thanks. Mel, can you give Stu his bath?"

Mel nods seriously, already looking like a little mother, and leads her brother off to the bathroom. She turns as she exits the room and says, "I'm an intelligent head too."

Jen laughs. "Of course you are dear, but someone has to look after Stu."

"OK," Jimmy starts. "We have a way to appear to strangers as if we are in the same room, without anyone else knowing about it. We have this climate change problem, and an organised denial campaign that won't go away. What can we do aside from targeting ringleaders of the campaign and making them think they're going crazy?"

"Not such a bad idea," Lukas mumbles, "except they're already crazy and no one pays attention." He is not looking his best.

"Are you OK, Lukas?" Jen asks.

"Fine, well actually, feeling a bit tired. Maybe go to bed and let you guys work it out for now. I'm really only good on the physics.

They toss ideas around, break for dinner and putting the kids to bed, then decide to call it a night. Jimmy wakes up a few times hearing someone go to the bathroom. Next morning, at breakfast, Lukas says, "I hope I didn't wake anyone up but I was in a bit of a sweat, almost felt like a fever, so I kept drinking water, but it's gone now. Did you guys come up with something?"

Jimmy shakes his head. "It's going to take some creative thinking. We shouldn't rush into anything, risk overplaying our hand."

They are still mulling over this a few days later, when Jen spots an angry lump on Lukas's forehead. "What happened to you?"

"Dunno. Think I've been bitten by a spider or something. Do you have spiders here with venomous bites?"

Jen says, "I don't know. I've only lived here a few years, but I haven't heard of anyone having a problem. Let's take you off to the doctor."

The doctor doesn't think it's a spider bite, and recommends a mild antiseptic cream. But Lukas looks steadily worse as they go to the pharmacy and apply the cream, though he insists on going back to the lab.

Nooby eyes him out. "You look a bit unsteady. Are you sure you shouldn't be at home in bed, maybe visit the quack again?"

"Nothing I can't handle. I'm getting behind."

"Well, I'm taking a lunch break. I need some air. Can I bring you something?"

"Not really hungry." Lukas dismisses him with a forced wave.

Nooby gets back and finds Lukas passed out on the floor. An hour later, Nooby, Jimmy, Jen and the kids are at Lukas's bedside at Stanford Hospital, cables and tubes all over the place. A couple of white-coated doctors arrive, and check a battery of instruments. Jimmy confronts them. "What exactly is going on? My friend had something that looked like a spider bite, now he's in a coma. The GP said it wasn't a spider. What is it?"

One of the doctors looks over his clipboard. "That's what we're trying to determine. Brain function makes it look like a minor stroke, but circulation is fine. Has he been exposed to infections lately? Travelled somewhere in the tropics?"

"Well, he was exposed to chicken pox about 6 weeks ago, but nothing happened."

"Chicken pox? Could be something. Sure he wasn't

exposed again? Once one of the children has it, it gets passed around."

"We did have some kiddy parties since, but no one had it."

"Can't be so sure. It's infectious before the symptoms show."

"Can you test for that?"

"Certainly. But the anti-viral drugs we have are not very effective unless you catch it early."

Jen chimes in. "But...chicken pox? I knew it could be more serious in adults than children, but how could it cause a stroke?"

Another of the doctors speaks up. "If the infection gets into the brain, it certainly can cause a stroke. Although it's rare, it's one of the leading causes of juvenile strokes."

They are all sitting in a daze in a waiting area, as the doctors carry on working on Lukas. The kids pick up the sombre mood of the adults, and are uncharacteristically quiet. After an hour, one of the doctors shows up. "Well, some good news. Brain function doesn't appear to be severely impaired. The scans show minor lesions in the speech area, so he may have a little difficulty talking, but motor control shouldn't be severely affected."

"And cognition?" Jimmy isn't sure what affects him more: the possibility of losing his weirdest friend, or losing his fantastic physics skills.

The doctor chooses his words carefully. "We really cannot say for sure until he wakes up. There's no real reason for him to be in a coma, probably a transient condition. He could even have bumped his head when he fell, though there's no obvious bruise or lump."

Half an hour later, the doctor returns. "He's awake. His words are a little slurred. Have you all already had chicken pox?"

They all nod, and Jen adds, "Lukas was the only one who hadn't had it when Stu picked it up." They follow the doctor back to the bedside.

Lukas smiles weakly. "Told you it was a s-spider."

"No Lukas, chicken pox." Jimmy looks at the doctor who led them in. The look on his face says Lukas has been told this.

The next few weeks are a trial. Lukas is soon well enough to be let out of hospital, but has great difficulty remembering anything. He recovers his physical strength soon, and his speech is only slightly affected, but he can't make any progress on his physics. He takes to writing notes to himself, which helps with the memory problem, but he arrives home each night totally frustrated and angry.

Then one night, his mood lifts. After Jen sends the kids to clean their teeth, she turns around and finds him still looking cheerful. "Lukas! Welcome back. We've all missed you so."

He looks around, animated as never before. "Sorry, I don't think I am back. Don't-don't know if we'll ever get me back. Can't get a handle on the physics anymore. Can't remember shit. But I have an idea."

24   The Lukas Trick

JIMMY HOLDS LUKAS'S HAND. It feels warm, alive. His eyes are animated, yet when he speaks, Jimmy knows the old Lukas really isn't there. "Lukas, let's hear your idea then."

Lukas grins. "We-we've been trying to be too clever, trying to think of ways we can use the technology to the max. All we need is a way of confusing the hell out of people by being in too many places at once, or near enough at once. Someone like me who can't remember shit, imagine we crash a conference of deniers, the kind they keep running, and I keep introducing myself to people, forgetting I talked to them before, and one of them eventually gets fed up and punches me out, hitting thin air. We can get the whole bunch of nutters completely certified insane. No need for me to be on the other side of the planet. I could even physically be there, carry the calibration machine around with me the first day of the conference, physically introduce myself to people, so it's even more weird."

Jimmy contemplates. "Interesting. Even if it's not physics, you are still the ideas man."

Jen looks a bit more doubtful. "But Lukas, I seem to recall an odd sensation in my head when Nooby appeared in my bedroom the first time. I didn't know what it was at the time, but won't people notice that and connect it with your weird appearances?"

"Maybe. But our job is to counter confusion with confusion. If-if they start talking to the public about funny visitations, and funny sensations in their heads, and no one but hard-core climate deniers have these things, they will get labelled as nutters. We can even throw in some flying saucer myths or other junk for them to repeat to make their experience even weirder."

They talk late into the night, periodically searching for denier conferences, refining ideas, laughing as they repeat stuff for Lukas. Finally they are all tired, and Jimmy looks serious. "Guys, I wonder if we should start looking at applications for my new long life theory, like fixing damaged brain cells."

Everyone else freezes, except Lukas, who nods slowly. "Yeah, happy to be the g-guinea-pig. But let's try this thing, my... my whatsit."

"Idea!" Jen shouts, loud enough to wake the dead, then a look dawns: "Damn, we didn't put the kids to bed."

They rush off to the kids' bedrooms, and Stu is sound asleep, clutching his teddy, and Mel is sitting up in her bed, reading light still on, looking stern. "Mom, you are not a responsible parent. I'm not supposed to give Stu his bath and put him to bed all on my own."

"I'm sorry, dear."

Mel still looks stern. "Unca Lukas has an excuse, he's

brain-damaged."

They all laugh, and Mel caves in and joins in.

Over the next week, the plan is refined. There's a conference run by a right wing think tank next month in Boston, and it's September, when the weather is great and fall leaves are an attraction. And the list of speakers is a who's who of climate change denial, everyone from a few otherwise-respectable academics who aren't embarrassed by the company they keep to outright cranks. "OK," says Jimmy, "it's not terribly expensive, so let's all go. We can flit in and out of sessions, get signatures from random people, mainly the bigwigs, but a few others to sow chaos, be inconspicuous, except Lukas. Stay in a neighbouring hotel, just to be safe." He looks around. "Remember the plan, Lukas?"

"What? Oh, yeah, yes, in general terms. Just remind me what I'm supposed to do." Jimmy looks sullen. "Got you!" Lukas grins widely.

So Jen and Jimmy are ensconced in a nice, not too fancy hotel room with the kids, and Nooby and Lukas have adjoining rooms. The fall leaves are all they're reported to be; after unpacking and a brief sojourn in the rooms, they all head out for a walk. Boston is full of pedestrians. Massachusetts Avenue, Mass Ave to the locals, is a mass of people. They find a coffee shop, and Jen and Jimmy keep the kids entertained while Nooby and Lukas order coffees and bagels. They return with a tray of cups and return for a second round with steaming hot toasted bagels in a range of flavours.

"The calm before the storm," says Lukas.

"Whaddayamean calm?" mutters Nooby, trying to keep track of which bagel is his while the kids cavort around.

The conference is in a smart hotel, not far from their more modest lodgings. Day one is predictably boring, dominated by opinionated pontificating windbags whose grasp of physics is seriously deficient, highly annoying Lukas. At the end of a coffee break when everyone else has headed into the next session, he corners Nooby and Jimmy. "Listen to those dolts. I-I'm supposed to be brain damaged but I can walk through the holes in their arguments."

Jimmy nods. "OK, but never mind that. Have you all got signatures of a good sample? I have about a dozen, most of the speakers including some talking tomorrow, a fair number of the audience. I had to look inconspicuous but still get their names off their name tags, not as easy as I thought."

Lukas says, "About the same. I think I got all the names."

Nooby looks contemplative. "I wonder what would happen if we had two slightly different quantum signatures for the same person. Could we lock onto them twice from different sources? Would locking on to different signatures for the same person at different times feel different?"

Lukas squints. "G-good questions. Wish I could answer. Let's compare lists at the end of the day and make sure we cut out duplicates. Chances are we will all catch some of the more conspicuous clowns: guest speakers and so on."

Jimmy prods him. "Lukas, now don't forget, also talk to people. You're the one going to show up in their heads."

"Oh, right. Forgot that. I mean who I talked to. I sound l-like a complete flake." He grins. "Plan working."

Nooby says confidentially, glancing around to make sure no one will hear how he's about to describe them, "Lukas, lad, you are not a flake in *this* company."

That night, they congregate in Nooby's room, while Jen puts the kids to bed. There are big overlaps in the lists of names, particularly the speakers, as Lukas predicted. Lukas is looking animated. "OK, so do we start now?"

Jimmy looks at him calmly. "Well, why not? I saw a couple of the bigwigs heading towards the hotel bar when we left. They presumably won't be driving after that, or at least shouldn't. So we shouldn't catch one in a life-threatening situation if we confuse him. Nooby, I think these are the names. Can you set one of them up?"

"My pleasure."

There follows a strange one-sided conversation, with Lukas doing all the talking. "Remember me?... Talked to you in a break I think... Cornelius Whiterspoon... From Australia... Just wondering, do you know what statistically significant means?" He signals cut at Nooby.

Nooby flips a switch. "How did that go?"

"The other guy with him kept answering when he asked me questions. Then I answered. And finally, when I asked him about statistical significance, he started ranting on, and when I asked Nooby to cut, he was looking away from me, so it would be as if I walked away, except his buddy didn't see me."

Jimmy smacks him on the back. "I would love to have seen how it looked to others around them. What's this Cornelius Whiterspoon from Australia?"

"Did I say that?" Lukas looks wide-eyed innocent. "I made that up as I went along. Make up something else next time."

Nooby contemplates. "You know, I think it will work best

if one of us goes to the conference tomorrow, and spots good opportunities, and sends Lukas in. He could for example start talking to the speaker just before a session starts, and get him hopelessly confused."

Jimmy nods. "Yup. But clue Lukas in on context to some extent, since he won't see what's going on from his side. How fast can you type on your phone?"

"Pretty fast."

"OK, so maybe it's a 2-person job. I spot opportunities from the back and message Nooby. Nooby types into the phone to message Lukas while I look for another mark, and Lukas jumps in when we say go. We can get this pretty seamless. Hit a new one before the last one has stopped ranting. And switch roles when the Nooby typing thumb gets tired."

Jen walks in at that point. "As usual, I miss all the fun."

Jimmy looks guilty. "Sorry my love. You don't like this techie stuff. Tomorrow, Nooby and I are going to spot opportunities for Lukas, who will be hanging out in his hotel room, to do weird visitations. What would you like to do?"

"Looks like I'm relegated to child minder. Again."

"Really, just this once. I think we should only do this for the one day, then clear out, in case someone twigs as to who Lukas really is. Since we aren't at the main conference hotel, no one should notice if we check out early."

25 Showdown

IT'S PANDEMONIUM. At session after session, Nooby and Jimmy alternate spying from the back and passing messages back to Lukas, who's in Jimmy and Jen's room where there's more space for equipment. Every now and then they take a break and find a quiet place to compare notes, taking care not to be seen.

At the afternoon coffee break, there's a weird buzz. Nooby walks past Jimmy as if he's a random stranger, then gives him a look. "Say, did you notice anything weird in your session? I didn't see you in mine. The speaker suddenly started talking to thin air."

"Strange." Jimmy looks up from picking up a coffee cup. "Someone in the audience in my session started ranting at no one in particular. I wonder if I should drink this? Maybe someone spiked the water?" *Why is Nooby talking to me? What happened to "inconspicuous"?*

Jimmy turns to his neighbour at the coffee table, a portly greying man, who has taken no food or coffee, but is eyeing the donuts. "Have I seen you somewhere before? Maybe in the media somewhere?"

"Yes, I'm Bob Cameron, climate scientist from Australia. I'm speaking next session. What were you saying to your friend about someone strange, about spiking the drinks?" He looks very suspicious.

Jimmy wonders if Cameron is onto him – things suddenly feel less tightly under control – but keeps calm. "Well I've been hearing strange things about behaviour of speakers and delegates. Did you notice anything?"

"Not particularly. I've been checking my slides. But if you are planning on your own private venture to track down what's going on, don't bother. The organizers have world-class security. They anticipated childish pranks by green lefties. You shouldn't worry, we'll be perfectly safe." He grins ambiguously.

Again, that uneasy feeling that things might be slipping out of control. *Cameron? Have I heard that name before? If he's just a scientist, if one who's sold out to commercial interests, surely he won't be involved in "security" whatever that is? Stupid Nooby, why did he talk to me?*

Jimmy nods and smiles tightly. "Good, I feel safer already. But not from the need to go to the bathroom." He uses the American term for a toilet, conscious that Australians may have a different usage, and backs away, his bladder suddenly feeling full at the turn of events.

He heads for the toilets. Nooby meanwhile is nowhere to be found. Jimmy heads outside to catch some air, when his phone beeps its message ready tone. It's from Jen. "Just back at room. Isn't Lukas supposed to be here?"

He checks his watch: coffee break almost up. Lukas could have ducked out for a coffee but he shouldn't still be out so he messages back: "Stay there I'll be right back. Call Nooby in."

He sprints the two blocks to the hotel, feeling hot eyes on his back the whole way. *Damn Nooby. Did he blow our cover? Why have we been so amateurish dealing with these people who stand to lose billions?*

He rushes through the foyer and rather than wait for the lifts runs up two flights of stairs. Jen is there waiting as he opens the door. The room looks just as they left it earlier, except for the absence of Lukas. Young Mel is comforting Stu, both looking a little tearful. The Nooby machine is still there, as is Lukas's phone that he uses to control the interface. A couple of minutes later Nooby appears, looking hot and red-faced from exertion.

Jimmy rounds on him. "Why did you talk to me? How was that part of keeping inconspicuous?"

Jen pulls him back from Nooby. "There's no time for that. It looks as if Lukas went without a struggle, at least not from here. Maybe we should try calling his phone before we jump to conclusions but I am inclined to go straight down to reception and ask if anyone saw him go out. I'll wait here with the kids but don't leave us alone for long. I don't want them to see what I'll do if the people responsible show up."

Jimmy pulls out his phone as they head out, and Lukas's phone goes straight to voice mail.

At the lobby, Nooby walks up to the counter and asks the clerk, "Do you remember my friend, the one with slightly hesitant speech?"

"Oh yes. He was lucky he had his personal doctor right there when he collapsed. Took him straight to his car, said he'd take him in for tests."

"He collapsed?"

"Yes. He walked past me towards the café." The clerk points at the coffee shop at the other side of the lobby. "Sat right there, ordered a cappuccino, drank a bit and keeled over. His doctor was sitting down right next to him as it happened. I went over to check he was OK. Why didn't you guys make sure you had his meds sorted if you can afford to bring your own doctor on a trip?"

The clerk looks annoyed and Nooby is about to protest when Jimmy restrains him. Jimmy says to the clerk: "Did the doctor say where he was taking him?"

"Why don't you ask him yourself?"

Jimmy ushers Nooby back to their room and reports to Jen, then adds: "Well of course if he's our friend's personal doctor, we would know how to find him, wouldn't we? Bastards. They think we can't report them to the cops because we are up to something. Well, maybe we should. What do you guys think? It will draw attention to us but kidnapping is a serious crime."

Nooby is not impressed. "Now hold on a minute. Why didn't you tell the clerk the whole thing was bogus? We're wasting valuable time."

"I don't know, not sure if I trust him. Jen, do you disagree with calling the cops?"

"No. Let's do it. Fast. And think of a good reason that someone might have abducted Lukas."

"Easy. He came back last night and told us he'd annoyed some prize cranks attending the conference, and one of them threatened him. We don't know anything more than that because we didn't think it was serious and didn't ask. We can't tell the cops about the Nooby machine. Even if they believed it, we'd be at risk of unwanted attention from the government. Every government probably. And I doubt they'd believe it anyway, dismiss *us* as cranks."

Nooby and Jen exchange glances. Nooby nods. "OK. It's not really a lie. If that's all we have it seems fair that we don't know more, and can't slip up if questioned in detail."

Ten minutes later, a detective is in the room, just enough time for Nooby to move a few pieces of electronics out to the car.

The detective looks around suspiciously after Jimmy gives him the story. "So how do you know your friend has been abducted?"

Jimmy repeats the conversation with the clerk. "Why would someone claim to be his doctor and cart him off? How many people have personal doctors who travel with them?"

The detective nods. "Yes, that is a bit weird, not the sort of cover someone would normally use. What if there was a real doctor present who challenged him on some detail? I'll question the clerk, and see if we can get any leads. I'd appreciate it if you didn't leave town until I've had time to ask some questions.

"From what you say though I doubt very much he's a target of organised crime. This doesn't fit the pattern, and I can't see why anyone would value him as a target. Are you sure he doesn't have any enemies, owe anyone money, or have wealthy connections who could be milked for ransom?"

"Sorry, no." The seriousness of the situation is starting to hit Jimmy. Without explaining what's going, there's no way to make the cops take it seriously. On the face of it, Lukas is a most unlikely kidnapping target.

Over the next couple of days, the cops ask a few questions at the conference, but no one, it seems, remembers Lukas. Then Jimmy is sitting at a café near the hotel waiting for Nooby, when he realises someone is sitting next to him. Before he can react, a cool voice says, "Don't worry. I'm not your friend's doctor."

"That's a pretty clear admission of guilt."

"Of what? Disrupting a lawfully conducted conference? Your friend was obviously off his meds."

"Ah, so you did pay off the hotel clerk."

"Not quite as stupid as you look. You don't know what you're playing with. Tell us what your friend was doing and you may get him back."

The stranger disappears smoothly into a gap in the crowd. Jimmy jumps up but he's gone and half a minute later, Nooby shows up. "What's the matter Jimmo? You look pretty shaken up."

Jimmy explains the visitation.

Nooby sits down. "Let's get a coffee and think this through."

Nooby's espresso and Jimmy's cappuccino arrive. "OK, so they are obviously super-confident that they can't be touched. Otherwise why risk letting you see one of them, someone you maybe could identify?"

"Obviously well connected. The cops are just going through the motions. Someone must have got to them."

"Yup. So we should try something better."

"Right. Let's give it a try." They exchange glances and

finish their coffees. *Nooby has obviously learnt to be discrete. No one listening in would know what they were trying.* Jimmy glances around. If they have a tail he's good. Or she.

They make it back to the hotel room, and Jimmy adds: "What if there are bugs in the room?"

"Good point. I don't think the cops need us any more. Let's find Jen and the kids and get back home."

The trip back to California seems to take forever. They queue at airports, sit around waiting, time on the plane drags on and renting a car at the San Francisco airport seems to take longer than usual. But eventually they are back in Nooby's lab, and turning on the machine.

Nooby adjusts the controls. "The good news is I'm picking up his signature. The bad news is I'm picking up no consistent signal on the instruments, no clear communication, just heavily garbled thoughts. And some that are pretty painful. Then the instruments all go haywire and what I pick up in my head is white noise."

Jen looks worried. "Does that mean. . ."

"I don't know what it means. I think he's alive. Maybe unconscious. I've never had this before. Jimmy, I think we should take turns watching for signs of life."

"I agree. Jen, get some sleep. Nooby and I will work out shifts."

"What about me? He's my friend too, you know."

Nooby shakes his head. "We didn't calibrate the machine for you since we did that demo way back. Your quantum signature may shift over time so we need to recalibrate. That could take time. We've never used the machine on someone with such a break so we can't be sure."

Jimmy nods. "One of us needs to get some sleep, and you have a business to run."

Reluctantly Jen heads for bed.

The next morning, she finds Nooby and Jimmy still awake at the machine. "I thought you were going to work in shifts."

"We are," says Jimmy. We take it in turns trying to reach him on the machine. He waves at a display. "We're getting some sort of signal so he must be alive, but looking into a head that's not fully working is scary. You can't do it for long."

"Enough of you taking all the pain. Let me try," she says as Nooby takes off his headset.

Jimmy starts to protest but she grabs the headset. "We're all part of the same team, aren't we? Set this thing up for me. It didn't take that long the first time, and you're doing it pretty fast connecting to random strangers. No more excuses."

As it turns out there isn't much to change. Nooby looks thoughtful. "That's an interesting new data point. Though now I think about it, older Jimmy a thousand years off locked onto his younger self, so there can't be too much drift."

In the meantime Jen is looking horrified, but pushes Jimmy away when he tries to intervene. "No, I'm doing my turn. And I see just what you mean. Poor Lukas. I hope he really is not aware of this. Did you know he felt hurt and betrayed by someone he trusts?"

Nooby shakes his head. "He was always so cool about people. Relationships didn't seem to touch him except that one time. And I had to say that stupid thing about Esmerelda. I can't believe the feelings I'm picking up. I wish I'd known about this before, we've been so focussed on fixing Jimmy. I'm sure we could have done something for him, whatever it was. I don't know what the brain dump from older you was like, but this is pretty rough."

The day wears on with no one relaxing much. Jen insists that Jimmy and Nooby at least take cat naps, and the kids try to do their part by looking serious and helping with making food. That night, they do take shifts, with two awake and sharing duties while the other sleeps for four hours.

Next morning Nooby makes coffees and brings them over to Jimmy and Jen, Jimmy on the machine, and finally there's a breakthrough.

26   Trapped

IT is dark. This much Jimmy can make out. He calls out to Nooby: "We have Lukas back. I think." Nooby rushes over and checks the readouts, as Jimmy concentrates on what he can sense through the connection.

Nooby frowns. "As long as there's a brain with his quantum signature, we have a connection. The readings are much the same as when trying to connect to him just felt like white noise. What's different for you?"

Jimmy holds up an index finger. *Lukas, are you with us? What's happening?* Vague sounds appear in the background. Nooby perks up, and raises a thumb, indicating readings looking better.

I think I'm with you. A bit groggy. Strapped to a table or something. Things start to appear in shades of grey, the usual fuzzy impression you get through the Nooby machine, sharpening up as the brain-brain connection improves.

Anyone with you? He repeats this aloud to Nooby.

Don't think so. Wait, I hear a door. Vague sense of a face. Jimmy hears an echo of Lukas's voice, interspersed with thoughts directed his way: *Esmerelda. What are you doing here?... Says she's as surprised as me. I don't believe you.... Says she was hired by this firm to do PR, brought here without any mention of me.*

Where's here? Esmerelda, you must know... did they drug you or something?

Why did she show up on the farm?

Let me deal with this. Remember, she can't hear you. Says she...

Nooby is fiddling with the settings, and suddenly things become clearer to Jimmy. **Lukas, I can make out what she's saying.** Suddenly he's in the scene in a way he hasn't been before.

"...you must think I'm so terrible, walking out on you, then this."

Lukas is talking to her, the sounds weirdly feeling as if Jimmy's making them. "OK, before you make me all judgmental over this, let me tell you a story. My parents got on like a house on fire. A lot of smoke and flames, and neighbours calling the emergency services. Well, not quite the latter. When I was, I don't know, fifteen or so, after my parents had a flaming row, and my mother is just about in tears, I ask her if she wants me to deck him. Me, a scrawny teen. 'Why?' she asks. 'Just look at you, I say, putting up with all that abuse.' She looks at me as if I'm crazy, then says, 'Never talk to me about the love of my life like that again.' Thing is, it took me a while to figure out, she just was totally non-judgmental about him. One time, she was complaining about his behaviour to a friend, I think it was one of her oldest friends, and this guy starts talking buddies who are divorce lawyers, and she never talked to him again."

Esmerelda looks puzzled. "You mean you think it's OK, what happened, what these people are doing?"

"Judging and being judgmental are not the same thing. Learnt that being judgmental is not the best thing. Though I think mum took it to an extreme. In fact, I think she was rather judgmental about her old friend. What you did, I don't want to judge. I think you had reasons. I may be right, maybe not, but you seem to me a pretty troubled person, and this isn't the time to sort that out. But definitely not judgmental about you. What these guys are doing, I don't think I will get the option. If I did, I would say they've taken advantage of you, and that adds to the list. So why did you walk out on me like that?"

"I made a stupid mistake. When I realized you had to find out, I couldn't face it, not hurting you like that." Esmerelda is looking at her feet.

Jimmy senses a grimace on Lukas's face. "If we had time we could work all this out. That was something I could easily understand, easily forgive. That's what my whole judgment spiel was about. But forget all that. What the hell is going on now? Why did you show up at the farm?"

"Showing up at the farm was a coincidence. I couldn't have relationships, just drifted. Was going with a friend by car to Cape Town, when he showed up, Nooby, as I was packing my stuff in the car at the B&B in Hanover. Stopped with Nooby for a coffee, and went home with him. I didn't recognise Nooby. Was he a friend of yours when we were together? Anyway. It totally freaked me when you showed up, and when Jimmy appeared, looking all moody like he was hiding stuff from that loving wife of his, it was all too much. I walked out, must have walked for hours in the cold before dawn, when a kindly old black man in a rickety car stopped and picked me up. He didn't stop lecturing me about people who get raped and in all kinds of trouble all the way to Hanover, where he dropped me off. Spotted someone checking out of a B&B, not the one where I was staying, implored him to give me a lift to Joburg, and tried to get on with my life. Then these guys showed up a year or so back and offered me this really great job and here I am. They must have somehow heard about my time at the farm and linked me with you. I am so, so sorry."

"Can you get me out of here?"

"I doubt it. This place is so locked down. I don't know how you're strapped in. They want to know what was going on at the farm. I couldn't help them."

"This is the tough part. I had a bout of chicken pox. Caused a stroke. Mostly recovered but can do bugger all physics. Equations a total blur. And all our work is back there at the farm. The other guys do not understand it all, just make stuff to my spec. For fear of the bad guys getting their hands on this, they may be forced to destroy everything, maybe send a coded message to security to torch the place. No way they can rebuild without me, without my specs. All gone if it comes to that."

Lukas! What are you doing? They will be listening.

I know what I'm doing. Listen and learn.

"Did they tell you what we've been up to?"

"Sort of. Something like talking inside people's heads."

"That's just a party trick, not our real project. Some MIT people came up with a cool idea, an audio spotlight. You can focus a beam of sound so tightly, only one person can hear it. The rest is just smoke and mirrors: your eyes play tricks on you when your senses are confused. We set that up in advance in a couple of places at a denialist conference. Really drove a couple of hard-core deniers crazy, worth the fun. Our real project is a trick that lets us look into the future. That's why we are taking on the deniers.

We all know that's impossible.

They don't. It'll keep them busy for years. No reputable physicist can be told how they found out and the other kind won't have the smarts to do more than milk them for money trying to do the impossible.

Nice touch, the audio spotlight. Just plausible enough.

Stop interrupting. Got to talk.

"You looked into the future? What did you see?"

"We have twenty years tops to turn around climate change. Then, big disasters. Not a one or two degree increase. A massive chunk of the West Antarctic slides into the sea. Big tsunamis, every coastal city flattened."

"If you could foresee that, why didn't you foresee getting caught like this?"

"You can't look everywhere at once. And the closer you are to an event, the fuzzier it is, because you can change it. I really wish I wasn't so damn brain damaged. I just can't understand this stuff any more."

"And you really can't tell anyone how to build this machine without the stuff on the farm? Why can't they just let you go?"

A door opens. A voice in the background. "Thanks, that's all we need to know."

What's happening?

They dragged Esmerelda off. Let me talk to them.

"Don't you care about civilisation as we know it ending in little over twenty years?"

Muffled voice: "Don't think so. Not in my lifetime."

"What if you could live longer, a lot longer?"

"What if we could? Not going to happen."

"Don't you care about your kids? Grandchildren?"

"Hate them with a passion."

Looks like they are going to inject something, and I don't think it's a party drug. I put them off the trail. Let them have the option to do the right thing but they are so greedy. Score now, to hell with the future. Being able to see into the future is a competitive advantage for them, not a tool to head off catastrophe. Get Kobus to make it look like we're trying to destroy our big secret, leave enough false trails for them to work off. Didn't mention his name, he should be safe if he watches himself.

Lukas! Where are you? We have to help you.

No time. Injecting now. No more getting into their heads. Keep our real secret weapon for us. Need new idea. Remember Rubber Duck. Do it for the kids. Do it for... tickle... monster ... and tell Esmerelda... knew what she was up to with my roommate all along... shouldn't have run...

Roommate? You mean your old bud going all the way back to kindie? Lukas!

Everything suddenly goes blank, not even white noise. Jimmy whips around to look at the instruments. They are all flatlining.

27   Cleaning Up

IT'S so brilliant, Lukas all over. Jimmy doesn't know whether to laugh or to cry, and tries both. *The MIT audio spotlight is a real concept, and the fact that no one will ever find the equipment we would have needed to set it up will only convince the bad guys how clever we are. We really will phone "security" and order a total destruct, but only after a delay, so it looks plausible. And Lukas is – was – absolutely right: he has tested these people by offering them the option of averting a bad future, and they have let greed drive them instead to chasing after an impossible machine.*

Jimmy uses the Nooby machine to warn Kobus, a step that gets them ahead of the game. **Kobus, we've lost Lukas.** He explains haltingly as far as he knows what happened.

He feels Kobus's sympathy deeply in his head, a new thing for him. *I didn't spend a whole lot of time with Lukas. I just didn't get what he was talking about, and I looked after my own shit. But I know how close you guys were. I'm really sorry.*

Jimmy collects himself. **Look, we will give you a call some time tomorrow, something that sounds like a coded** *message. That will panic them into moving. Meantime set up a fireworks show. The whole place should go up, but maybe a few bits don't actually burn. Make it convincing enough that they think we were serious but did a rush job. Doesn't really matter what they recover, it's all junk.*

OK boss. I can set up a bunch of fuses with varying times, a few a little faulty. When do I set it off?

Ideally just before they arrive so they have a chance of stopping it, but no way must you risk getting caught.

No problem. I'll get my guys out as soon as possible, set the thing up and watch from the koppie, set it off by remote.

Be careful. These guys can afford the best kit, IR scanners and so on.

Don't worry. There's a big rock up there I can hide under, they won't see me from above. I have time to prepare, and they will be in a hurry.

Then next morning, Jimmy, Nooby and Jen are sitting together at home, all with signs of no sleep. "OK," says Jimmy. "Enough time. Let's give Kobus his coded message." Nooby nods. Jimmy looks to Jen. No one disagrees. He lifts the phone. "Security? Head office here. It seems the eagle has landed. Time for plan B." He can visualise Kobus on the other end, grinning at the inanity of the secret message, but no one here feels any levity.

Jen is staring straight ahead. "Never mind the farm. How are we going to tell the kids about their tickle monster?"

Jimmy puts a hand on her shoulder. "He said something about rubber duck, I think that book you were reading. He said we should do it for the kids, for the tickle monster."

Jen nods. "I think I know what he meant. One of the

things the activists did in the book was taking a bunch of young mothers with babies to a politician's office by way of protest. They had the law changed in record time."

"We only have one youngish mum and no one quite a baby." Nooby is looking a bit more shocked than the others, reality finally sinking home.

Jimmy helps him. "We have truckloads of money, and there's a new invention, social networking. We need to beat the other side at their game. Create a grassroots movement using social networks, something like mothers against denial, MAD."

Nooby looks doubtful. "I think that acronym's been used."

"Who cares? It's good. Let's get our PR machine onto it. Make it MAD^2. Make sure everyone knows it's pronounced 'mad-squared'."

So the MAD^2 campaign begins. Shortly into it, Kobus and the crew show up, making for a full house. Introductions are brief. "Guys, I think some of you have met Memela."

Jimmy shakes Memela's hand. "We had some good discussions back on the farm. Who's this? I recognise you but you kept to yourself."

"Johnson."

"OK, still keeping to yourself. Is that your only name?"

Kobus intervenes. "He's had a difficult history. I'd trust these two guys with my life, otherwise they wouldn't be here."

Jimmy looks from Kobus to Johnson and back. "OK, so another single name. If you want to tell your story, that's up to you. We work on trust here. If Kobus knows he can trust you, I hope he's right."

Johnson shows no expression on a face that might as well be carved from granite. "Trust works for me." Kobus looks pointedly at Jimmy and the conversation ends.

The first few weeks are bedlam as PR consultants, young mothers with screaming babies and computer consultants show up to launch the campaign. Then it goes viral and every politician in every free democracy around the world – and even some less free – gets to learn the limits of their power.

In Australia, South Africa and England, pram parades clog the streets. In the US and Canada, stroller sit-ins block access to public buildings. Members of the US congress and various parliaments around the world are accosted by groups of mothers with angry babies.

And as this all becomes increasingly frantic for politicians and special interests, the Anderson household returns to a semblance of normality, with the very empty space that is Lukas still hard to ignore.

After yet another evening news of angry protests around the world, Jimmy helps put the kids to bed, then calls everyone together. "Guys, this is fantastic, but we are forgetting the other small detail: alternatives. I've been checking my stock portfolio and we can easily spend a few billion on jump-starting a couple of industries. The question is: which? Nooby, as our surviving physicist, any ideas?"

"Not really, no. We need to research this. What criteria should we use? Potential impact? Likelihood of getting to market?"

"I would say both. Rank all solutions on both scores, then pick some winners. Then we launch a company to partner with anyone out there we can work with."

"As the non-technical member of the team," Jen adds, "can I propose a company name? How about Lukas Energy?"

Jimmy shakes his head. "I like the idea but I think there's already an appliance or component company called Lucas. British. Car headlights and things."

"How about Tickle Monster Technology?"

Jimmy stares at Jen. "Brilliant. We know what it means but no one else does. And why do we care if no one else knows? It's *our* money."

So TMT becomes a registered trade mark of Tickle Monster Technology, and anyone who asks gets a Mona Lisa smile. If they press further, they get told it has to have a different name to GenInTel because it's a totally different product line. A few business journalists mutter about shareholders not appreciating a British sense of humour, and Jimmy ends the conversation by pointing out that they aren't British, they aren't a listed company and no one has to understand their humour, or whatever else is behind the name.

28   Esmerelda

THINGS ARE STARTING to get hot.   Jimmy searches Greek island ads, and some look promising so he dispatches Kobus to scope them out. While all this is happening, the rest of Kobus's crew establish themselves in Jimmy's house, and the whole thing feels a bit conspicuous. There aren't many Palo Alto households with three hangers-on with a distinctly military bearing and panther-like reflexes.

Jimmy and Jen are lying in bed after another hectic day. He touches her hair. "What happened about our old low profile?"

"They're onto us now. If we retire to the island, whichever one Kobus thinks is good, we will be more isolated but they know who we are now, and know we're behind all the protests."

"So no more quiet life."

"The island will be pretty quiet if we want it that way. And I think we do, don't we? The latest report from Kobus is pretty good, there are plenty to choose from, all easy to secure, and some with nice houses that would suit our needs."

They drift off to sleep slowly, and Jimmy wakes up a few

times, relieved to see each time that Jen is still asleep. Next morning, he offers to make cappuccinos to get the day off to a start. She takes a look at him and says, "No, you stay here. You get brekkie in bed for a change." She ignores his protests that she doesn't know how to work the cappuccino machine, and returns an indeterminate time later with a tray of croissants and preserves.

"I didn't know you could make croissants." He says nothing about cappuccinos.

"Didn't," she said. "Memela went out and got them for me. Might as well use the help."

"What about Nooby? Is he up yet?"

"No sign of activity from his room. We might as well have a late day and rebuild some energy. Jane is looking after the kids, and they're playing nicely in the back yard."

"Don't you need to get to the shop?"

"I've got help for that too, remember. I gave them a call. The shop will run itself for a change."

After the luxury of extra snuggle time, they are eventually up and dressed, when the doorbell rings. Jimmy goes to the door with Memela in the background, a casual but reassuring presence.

It's Esmerelda.

She looks as if she hasn't slept in a week. Jimmy lets her in wordlessly, not sure what to say, exchanging glances with Jen. It doesn't take the Nooby machine to communicate: *she doesn't know we know.*

Memela susses the situation as well as he can, without inside knowledge of Esmerelda and her history, and announces he's off to do more shopping for the additional guest. Jimmy sits her down in the living room, and Jen brings in tea.

Esmerelda is having difficulty talking about anything but how she likes her tea (milk, no sugar) but no one is forcing the pace. After a few sips of tea she opens up a bit. "It's Lukas. They got him. I don't know if he's alive or dead."

Jimmy holds up a hand. "Just wait. We know he's been abducted. The cops in Boston seemed remarkably uninterested in pursuing the case. Who are 'they'? How do you know all this?"

Meanwhile Nooby's door opens, and he and Esmerelda share a protracted uncertain gaze.

"OK," says Jen. "Let's start that all again, and take it slowly. Esmerelda, what do you know? Is it something we can take to the cops? All we know is someone disappeared with him when we were in Boston, probably after bribing the hotel staff to look the other way and drugging him. We have pretty good resources to track him down, and found nothing."

Nooby sits down, looking a little shaken. Esmerelda looks no better for his presence.

Jen sits next to her on the couch. "Take it slowly."

Esmerelda takes a sip of tea. "I've been doing some work in PR, a new thing for me, but I was doing well. I set up office in Pretoria, and strangely enough there seems to be a lot of demand there, despite Joburg being the centre of the economy. Then someone approached me, said he was from a big US company, and they had a contract for me, could I come out to the States? I said OK, and they bought me a first class ticket to Dallas, and things got a bit hazy after that. I think I may have been drugged." She pauses. "That seems to be their thing. I'm not sure where I ended up. It was in a building with no natural light. I was totally disorientated, then they started asking me what you guys were up to on the farm. Eventually, they accepted that I really knew nothing. I was getting pretty desperate by then, and just wanted them to let me go, no questions asked, when they brought Lukas in."

Jimmy sits on the edge of his chair. "Is he OK? What did they do to him?"

"I really don't know. They had him strapped down using some sort of high-tech strapping. I couldn't work out how it was done, and they obviously didn't want me to help him to get loose. We talked about stuff, a lot of personal stuff, he didn't seem to care what slipped out. He wasn't himself, something badly wrong. He said something about chicken pox, brain damage. I was in quite a state, so I don't know if I have this all straight."

Jimmy nods and Nooby butts in: "So far, that sounds right. He had chicken pox. We kind of expected it, then forgot about it because he didn't get it on first exposure, probably from a kid who got it in the second round, and didn't treat it in time. It got into his brain and caused a minor stroke."

Esmerelda is looking even more miserable. "I wouldn't call it 'minor'. He wasn't his old self by a long way, and not just because he'd been drugged and strapped to the furniture."

Jimmy explains. "'Minor' means no paralysis or long-term physical incapacity. His speech was a bit affected at first, but that more or less came right. His memory was shot at first, though that got better. He couldn't do physics at all, a total blank. So I suppose for Lukas, it was pretty major."

Esmerelda nods. "I think he managed to convince the people who were holding us of that. He also said you have a device for looking into the future, and that seemed to make them happy, and that's about the last thing I know. I was very worried about what they were about to do to Lukas, but they pushed me out of the room and I didn't see him again."

At that point, she's in tears, and Jen tries to comfort her. "Guys, I think Esmerelda needs some quiet time to come to terms with whatever happened. I don't know if the cops will help at all if we feed them this extra information. Esmerelda, how about the two of us have a quiet chat, and Jimmy and Nooby can leave us to it? Then I think she needs a shower and a lie-down."

Jimmy and Nooby exchange glances. This seems like a good moment to compare notes based on their own understanding of the events while Lukas was detained – out of earshot of Esmerelda. Jimmy says, "As usual, you're right. Nooby, let's go to my lab to talk. We have some stuff to sort out."

Away from Esmerelda, Nooby says, "Her story pretty well checks out, and there's no way she'd know we were there. What do you think?"

"Right. If she was going to lie, she wouldn't know we could check the detail. I'm not sure though if that means we can trust her. Why did she show up here?"

"Good question. Maybe Jen will dig that out of her. My inclination is that the bad guys dumped her on us to rub our noses in how powerless we are, and to hint that Lukas may still be around."

"So what do we do?"

"Call their bluff. Let Esmerelda hang around if she wants to, but don't tell her anything we don't want them to know in case she's being used again, or will be in the future."

Jimmy smiles grimly. "We can always confuse them further with the facts if need be. Let's give Jen a bit more time, then see what she's found out. So much for a quiet day away from the office." He explains Kobus's last report-back on Greek islands, and the leisurely start to the day. "It seems it's a great time to buy up anything in Greece. That put us into a good mood, a leisurely state of mind. Didn't last long."

"Oh well, I'm sure there will be plenty more opportunities for that."

"I'm not so sure. If they dumped Esmerelda back here, maybe they're planning something and did this to put us off balance. We have to move. The hard part is convincing Jen. She's put so much investment into the community here, MAD^2, ... To me all that is just a strategy, and it will continue anyway without us. I'll have to work on her."

29   Get Packing

IT'S A BRIGHT SUNNY NORTH CALIFORNIA DAY. Jimmy, Jen, Nooby and Kobus are out on the deck, sipping fresh cappuccinos. Memela and Johnson are in the back yard, tidying the gardening equipment. Jimmy looks contemplative. "I think getting a top of the line Italian cappuccino machine is one of the best decisions I ever made."

Jen gives him a look. "Better than getting married to me?"

"Of course not darling. I mean choices like buying cars and so on. Why is it that the Italians can't make a car that doesn't fall apart, and no one else can make a cappuccino machine that works consistently and lasts forever with a little basic maintenance?"

"Speaking of choices," Nooby pipes up, "what about the plan to move to the island?"

Jimmy looks grim. "A tough move. The kids have all their friends here, Jen has her shop. Jen and I keep arguing about it. I think we should go before anything happens, but Jen thinks they would not be brazen enough to go after us in Palo Alto."

Jen says, "After all, Lukas did stick his head into the lions' den. Not that it justifies what they did, but if we keep a low profile, will they see us as anything different than before they went after Lukas?"

Kobus contemplates. "Ja, but these people have shown us what they can do. They showed contempt by sending Esmerelda back. I would be much happier in a place we can lock down. Jen, you don't want me around you all the time and I can't watch a whole town. Not even with Memela and Johnson to back me up."

Jen is unconvinced. "We launched our protest movement before all this happened. They did nothing. They think they have all they can get from us that Lukas knew. If Esmerelda has fed anything back to them, it can only confirm that."

The argument goes nowhere, and stops cold when Esmerelda walks out onto the deck. "What's the matter? Did I interrupt something."

"No, no," says Jimmy a little too quickly. "Just a break in the conversation. What's everyone's plan for the day? I think I'll do a bit of work on my clean energy portfolios, see if anything needs propping up."

Esmerelda as usual has no plans, and Jen is about to start out for the shop. "It's such a nice day, I think I'll walk." She looks pointedly at Kobus, who shows no reaction.

Nooby shrugs. "Looks like same old same old today. I'll get back to my physics, see if I can work out a new angle."

Kobus wanders off to the kitchen to get breakfast for his crew, and Jen gathers up her work bag and paraphernalia. Jimmy stays on the deck and gives her a good-bye kiss. "I hope it goes well today. Give me a call if you'd like me to fetch you."

"Shouldn't be necessary. Looks like another sunny day. One of the things I like about this place."

"In summer," he counters as she walks out to the street.

It's an easy 30 minute walk to the shop, and Jen's about a block away when she passes through a small deserted alley. Suddenly there are two men who've appeared from nowhere on either side of her. She looks around desperately but they've picked their spot well. No one can see them.

"Now listen carefully," one says, behind the anonymity of designer shades. "You know what happened to your buddy Lukas."

"No, I don't know."

"Well you can guess, and guess the same could happen again if you don't stop annoying some very powerful people."

Suddenly there is a forceful parting of the close space between Jen and her accosters. It's Kobus. "Now, you listen. Your bosses may have a lot of money but they don't have me. Get out of my sight."

He doesn't explain the options, and doesn't have to. The unwanted company is gone as quickly as it appeared. "Now are you so sure it's safe here?"

That night, Jimmy, Jen, Kobus and Nooby talk strategy. Jen is still a bit shaken but defiant. "Those people as much as admitted to doing away with Lukas. I heard them, and I'm pretty sure Kobus heard everything or at least most of it."

Kobus nods tightly. "I heard a bit and maybe it would stand up in court, but my focus was on getting rid of them not arresting them. I didn't think they would risk a public fight, so I took a chance on taking them on and anyway it's my job, and I do my job no matter what it takes. If they were armed or

well trained in combat, I couldn't have stopped them. But Jen
could still have run away and called for help. We could hire
a private detective agency to track them down but I wouldn't
give much for our chances. If their bosses have any sense
they would bring in an out of town team and recycle as soon
as their identity was at risk."

Jen turns on him. "So you say there's nothing we can do
but run?"

"Jen", Kobus says slowly, "I knew some very brave men
who didn't believe in running. I was very sad at their funerals.
I'm alive, they aren't. The cause they were fighting for turned
out to be a bad one, and I'm not saying that about your fight,
but you don't win if you're dead."

"OK," says Jen. "Let's start packing."

Nooby adds: "What about Esmerelda?"

"Good question." Jimmy turns to Kobus. "Would she add
to the risk if she was with us?"

"Not really. I don't clue her in on what I'm doing about
security, and we can always feed her false information in case
she's in with the other side. And if she's not, what would you
feel about leaving her to them?"

"Interesting." Nooby looks at Kobus with new respect. "I
always thought you tough military types did whatever it took
to look after yourself and those paying you."

"Ja. A lot of them are like that. I've seen that too much to
throw someone to the wolves. I can handle any problem she
causes and I'd rather have her close in case we can find out
more about the other side through her. And it keeps them
guessing too. Why *would* we take her with us? Is there
something she knows that they didn't get out of her?"

Jimmy grins, his mood lightening. "Guys, you don't know Kobus the way I do. Despite his apparent lack of sophistication he was the sweet voice of reason that made things bearable for me in the army. No one else sussed the system as well as he did. I was pretty idiotic and lucked out, and he picked up the pieces pretty quickly when luck went my way."

30 Trust

WHEN IT RAINS IN NORTHERN CALIFORNIA, it *rains*. They are a good way towards packing up the house, with professional movers operating under closer supervision than they obviously like. It's raining so hard that Jimmy orders a halt rather than have mud tracked into the house. They are sitting in a half-packed living room, couches still unwrapped. Kobus is with the family, his two sidekicks lurking in the garage checking through tools that haven't yet been packed.

"What should we do?" asks Jen. "We can't all just sit around moping about the rain."

"And it's too cold to go outside." Jimmy grins. "I know what. There's a dictionary they haven't packed yet. I know a game I haven't played since I was an undergrad."

He explains the rules. "One person has the dictionary, and chooses a word with an obscure definition, and reads out the word. Then everyone writes their definition, which can be completely made up, and passes it to the dictionary holder, who collects them all then reads them out. We all then vote on definitions, and you get a point for everyone who votes for your definition, and..." He pauses. "I'm trying to remember how the dictionary holder gets rewarded for confusing everyone, which is the point."

The family gets into a furious argument about how this could possibly work, Kobus watching bemused from the sidelines, and Nooby obviously in a different place. In the midst of this, Esmerelda stands up and says, "I'm sorry. My head is full. Cold rain or no, I'm taking a walk."

Before anyone can protest, she's out. Jimmy looks at Kobus. "Don't worry, one of the guys will follow her at a distance. She won't go walkabout again."

"On the subject of that, have we any indication we can trust her? I'm still not so sure about this plan of yours of just letting her tag along, and dealing with problems if they pop up."

Kobus looks at Jimmy levelly. "No, you're right. I've been thinking about it. Let's set up something, a test. We really ought to know before we go to our island. At least to the extent of basic trust, even if her personality is a bit flakey."

"What exactly do you have in mind?"

"Jimmy, I want this to look like a surprise when I mention it. So don't ask. OK?"

"Well, OK. Should we get back to the game?"

Jen looks thoughtful. "Do you think it can work like this? We all get a point for anyone who votes for our definition, and the dictionary person gets a point for everyone who votes for a wrong definition?"

"That sounds brilliant," says Nooby, whose attention suddenly returns to the moment. "Puts pressure on the dictionary person to choose a word with a really obscure-sounding definition. And the rest of us to come up with something that sounds like a real dictionary definition. And the dictionary must move after each word, so one person can't crack the system and get all the easy points."

Jimmy nods. "Jen, you should have been a scientist."

She laughs. "Not only scientists are logical. Anyway let's all play. Do I get the dictionary first since I worked out the rules?"

Kobus shakes his head as they pass writing pads around. "Sorry guys. I'll watch and learn. Words are not my thing."

Time passes pretty fast, and they are into the second round with the dictionary back at Jen. "How about this one? Zebra."

"Everyone knows what a zebra is," yells Stu.

Mel grins. "But mom doesn't have to use the obvious definition. Let's play."

Stu looks determined, and his sister holds his gaze. They all start writing, then pass their definitions to Jen. She reads them all out, and calls for votes on the first one, when the front door opens. It's a dramatic moment, Esmerelda darkly silhouetted against the bright grey of the cloudy sky, wind whipping her hair as she lowers her dripping hood.

Then she closes the door and says, "What's up? I'm not a ghost."

Jen laughs nervously. "I certainly hope not. Sorry, we were so into the game, the door opening was a shock. Welcome back. Would you like to join in? Maybe I can take a break and make cocoa, and you can take over my score."

"Yeah mom, make cocoa," yells Stu.

"Seems I don't get to choose," says Esmerelda, "as usual."

"Hey no," Mel looks at her sternly. "You did choose. You

went out in the rain. Choices have *consequences*. Mom, isn't that what you keep telling us? Going out in the winter rain has a *cocoa consequence*." Mel gives her a hug, and Esmerelda visibly lightens up, though still dripping a tad.

As Kobus takes her coat and finds her a towel, Jen disappears to the kitchen, and returns in few minutes with five steaming mugs. "The wonders of microwaves. How did you guys get on without me?"

"Not so great," says Esmerelda. "I don't have the knack of making things sound like dictionary definitions."

Kobus shows amusement for a change. "Esmerelda, you are nowhere near as useless as me at this. I know what I'm good at." He suddenly looks more serious than usual, a complete turnaround. "Oh crap. Not so good after all."

"What?" asks Jimmy.

"I forgot. The safe. When we cleaned out at the farm we were in such a rush, I forgot that I decided at the time that they wouldn't find the safe, and left it to pick up later."

"Safe?" asks Jimmy uncomprehending.

"Ja. I know you think Lukas didn't write anything down but I saw him put some notebooks in the safe, and I'm pretty sure they wouldn't have found it if they weren't looking for it."

Jimmy suddenly twigs. "Nooby, do you know if Lukas kept separate notes on the stuff he was thinking of that he didn't share with you?"

Nooby still looks puzzled. "I really don't remember anything like this. I mean obviously if he didn't show them to me I wouldn't know. Are you sure…?"

Kobus looks especially grim. "Ja of course I'm sure. It's

my job to notice everything, dammit. Look, if they didn't find
the safe first time around, they aren't going to go back, but I
think I should play safe and go back some time soon to check
on it."

Nooby is about to say something, when Jimmy intervenes. "Of course you should. But let's not make it look as
if you're rushing off so they suspect something if they're still
watching us. Nooby, maybe we should talk to Kobus about
what to look for, and not spoil the game for everyone else."
He ushers them out of the room to his study.

Nooby is still looking puzzled. "Brilliant," says Jimmy.
"I don't think she'd have cause to suspect a thing. Kobus,
you're a genius. Making it a real surprise means we didn't
have to act."

Now Nooby gets it. "Jeez guys. I'm so slow. Did I get
chicken pox and nobody told me?"

"Not funny." Jimmy used to admire Nooby for his sharp
wit. So much has changed. "Kobus, now Esmerelda knows,
let's give her some space to report in, if she *is* spying on us,
but not unnatural loss of protection. If these people are really
watching us, they would have to be pretty professional if you
haven't picked it up. Right?"

"Ja. My guys are pretty good, and we haven't seen
anything since that time they scared Jen, and we've been extra
watchful since. How's about next time I go to Greece to check
the island, someone suggests a diversion to SA to recruit more
security? That way it looks like a pretext to go to the farm and
if she's reporting back, they'll think they have to move fast."

"OK. What if they get there first?"

"No problem. I planted a safe behind some fake plaster

where you wouldn't think to look. But if you do look, maybe with a metal detector, you'll find it. Anyway we are moving out in less than a week, and it's a pretty natural thing for your security to go early to check things out. I already planned to go out a couple of times while the container is on the water to set things up. It will only seem out of the ordinary if someone tells them. They are probably at least as paranoid as us."

Nooby is trying to catch up. "You did what?"

"A decoy. I knew you guys were working on secret stuff, so I thought I should give them something to find. The safe will be damn hard to open so they will have to take it away with them, and they'll find it only has some old pieces of newspaper in it when they do open it. I have a few hidden cameras they didn't think to look for before, so we can see some of the action, until they think of looking for them and take them out, which could happen if they scan for RF signals while I'm accessing them. I check on them every now and then, and they still get solar power."

"That's if they actually show up." Nooby looks doubtful.

"Ja. This is a test of Esmerelda, not them, not so?"

"Well, what if they don't show up?"

"I leave the safe there. Who knows when we may need to leak the story again."

"And what do we tell Esmerelda then, if nothing happens?"

"I bring you some notebooks and you say they're worthless. In fact, I suggest you guys write some stuff in some notebooks now, and I produce them when I get back. You can fake sciency stuff. No way I can do that."

The next day is bright and sunny, and the movers are back,

and declare they need two more days to finish.

As they conclude discussion with the movers, Kobus says, "I should go to the island to do a final check up. Maybe stop on the way in SA to check on some other talent we may want to recruit."

"Aren't you going out a week ahead of us anyway?" Jen asks.

"Ja, but I've had some local contractors set up electronics and I want to check it before we all start traveling."

"Kobus, I guess we should be OK without you while staying in good hotels and resorts."

"Ja, if you don't wander off on your own too much." Kobus looks pointedly at Jen and Esmerelda.

As the container vanishes down the road, Jimmy feels that once again an era is ending. California has been good to him. TMT and GenIntel are still headquartered there. Dianne's parents are part of what makes Northern California feel like home. Taking a break at Yosemite with them seems like a good way of getting closure, but he suddenly feels for Dianne again in a way he hasn't in years. *And my Mel, so long gone...* he dismisses the thought.

They pile into cars and head for Dianne's parents, where there's a lot of hugging and tears at the prospect of parting. Then they all go inside, and find spaces for their luggage. In a couple of days, they are loading up into cars again. Memela drives the kids and Esmerelda in Jimmy's Lexus, and Jimmy insists on driving Steve's Lincoln. Johnson brings up the rear in Jen's Mazda with Nooby. Steve sits next to Jimmy, with Jen and Maddy in the back. "Just like old times," the old man says.

Jimmy smiles at Steve. "You must still miss Dianne a lot. I do too even though Jen and the kids are so important to me now."

"Yes. I'm glad they all became part of our lives. Our Di was so special to us that we can never replace her, though they do fill a gap. And you are still our boy."

Jimmy eases into the traffic, following Memela, who drives sedately, as if he hadn't learnt his craft in the crazy traffic of Joburg. "You know, our island is plenty big enough for you two, if you want to join us."

Maddy puts a hand on Steve's shoulder. "We've thought about that a lot. Steve and I would love to visit, but we have so many friends here. When you get to our age, that means a lot. We still do tennis Saturdays even if we can't play much any more, and that's more than a habit."

Jimmy suppresses a Mona Lisa half-grin. "Now, don't give me that 'we're old' talk. You aren't that old."

Conversation drifts to other things, nostalgia, future plans, what GenInTel and TMT will do in future. Jimmy is meanwhile trying to put out of his mind his general feeling of unease at not using their knowledge about ageing for people who really need it. *Time enough: they aren't so old that it's life and death and we need to be sure before experimenting on real people.* He focuses on driving the Lincoln, an odd experience for someone accustomed to the precision of premium European and Japanese brands.

"Son, what do you think of my car?"

"Dad, it's not what I'm used to. I have a few hours to learn."

"You don't have to humour me. It's what I grew up with.

My dad could only afford mass-market Fords, and aspired to getting a Lincoln. As soon as I could afford one, I bought one, and have stuck by them ever since. I'm sure someone who grew up with European and Japanese would have a different opinion and you're entitled to yours."

"Dad, having a parent whose aspirations you looked up to is something I sorely missed. I'll get used to this."

"The car?" asks Jen, obviously not paying close attention.

"No, what it represents."

At Yosemite time passes fast, with long walks leading to sound sleep at night, and they are all too soon heading back to Palo Alto. Back at Steve and Maddy's house, they off-load, and Memela soon after heads off to the airport to fetch Kobus.

Esmerelda meanwhile is unpacking and helping with the kids, showing absolutely no concern – a promising sign, Jimmy thinks. He corners Nooby when no one else is in earshot. "I can't see Esmerelda as being such a brilliant actor. She knew about the safe, and that Kobus was travelling. She'd have to worry what he found if she was spying on us and reported in ahead of his trip."

Nooby nods. "I think you're right. I can't see her hiding that level of stress, but let's see what Kobus has for us."

An hour later, Memela and Kobus arrive. As soon as Esmerelda goes to the bathroom, Jimmy takes Kobus for a walk in the garden. "Was the safe still there?"

Kobus looks thoughtful. "See, the thing is, there never was a safe. If they went looking for it they would have taken half the house apart."

"What about your cameras?"

"I had none, because there wasn't time to set up

something like that. Did you really think I was such a genius and set this all up as if I knew exactly what would happen? I put some cameras and sensors in now, so we'll know if anyone shows up. The best I could do now is check if there's any sign of new damage. After so much time, there's plenty of dust, and it wasn't disturbed. The bigger question is did she show any sign of suspicious behaviour?"

"No, not that I noticed, and Nooby knows her better, and saw nothing. So do we trust her?"

"I wouldn't say 100%, but I'm reasonably sure she isn't spying on us, not the way we suspected."

Jimmy stops. "Wait a minute. I don't remember you talking about all that detail in front of Esmerelda."

"True. But you have to have your whole story straight in case one of us starts talking details. Just knowing there was supposed to be a safe is all she needed."

They walk back inside as Esmerelda emerges from the bathroom and gives them an extra-pointed look. "So do you trust me now?"

Jimmy looks completely helpless and for the first time, she laughs. "*I* wouldn't trust me after what happened, and I must admit, you guys are good. If I hadn't been expecting some sort of test, I wouldn't have suspected. I'll tell you what. Don't tell me anything you wouldn't tell anyone else, and I'll work on giving you reason to trust me. I know it takes a lot to win trust back when you lost it, and it means a lot to me that you're giving me the option. I have no idea what I did to deserve that, but it really does mean a lot."

Esmerelda's mood swings. Almost in tears, she says: "If you guys knew what I did to Lukas…"

Jimmy puts a hand on her shoulder. "Esmerelda, don't worry about how we'll react. Tell us when you're ready. I'm not a real expert on this but the point of a cover-up is to put you in a better place than the truth, and you are obviously not in a good place right now. If you want trust, you have to trust us, OK? No one will push you but when you are ready, it would be better if you let it out."

Nooby's face works slowly, and he says: "One thing Lukas said that he never explained. He said to tell you he knew about Joe all along."

Jimmy's hand is still on her shoulder. He looks her in the eye. "It was one of the last things he told me. Before we... lost track..."

She bursts into tears, composure gone so suddenly it takes everyone by surprise. Jimmy sits her down, and she looks up at him. "You guys are so good to me, and I'm such a jerk. Joe was Lukas's oldest buddy, they went back to kindergarten, and it was such a stupid thing. I wasn't even in love with him, and I found myself so scared that Lukas would find out what we were up to, I ran away. And now I worry that my stupidity has killed Lukas."

Jimmy holds her. "We don't know with certainty that Lukas is dead, though things don't look good I must admit. And anyway whatever happened, you didn't do it. We all have our weaknesses. It's exploiting weakness that takes you to the dark side. I'm sure Lukas wouldn't want you miserable. Really sure."

"Funny. I don't know how you can be so sure, but I believe you." Esmerelda gets up. "I have a little packing to do."

Jen takes her arm. "Let me help," and leaves Nooby and Jimmy alone.

Nooby's eyes track them out of the room then he turns to Jimmy. "You know, that thing I said in the restaurant, that first day in Palo Alto, unsavoury tart..."

"I know. You have flappy mouth disease. You didn't mean it."

"But did Lukas know that?"

"You knew him better than I did. What do you think?"

"He forgave a hell of a lot. I wish I'd thought to say something. That's all."

"As long as you don't get like me, a thousand years of regrets and all that. The main point is, the only other person it could hurt is Esmerelda, so we keep it to ourselves."

Nooby nods, as Jen walks back in and takes in the scene. "Looks like you guys have been sharing your own special moment of packing something away."

31 Endgame

JIMMY is watching the news. Protests around the world are growing. Others are joining the mothers. MAD^2 is becoming more like MAD^3. TMT is growing rapidly as it's becoming clear that real clean technologies will be the only option. But still, he feels something is missing. Nooby and Jen are there, and he turns off the TV.

Nooby grabs for the remote. "Hey! I was watching that. We're going pretty well."

"Well, but not well enough. We are on track for clean energy at about half the level we need in the next decade. I keep thinking I'm missing something, something in that last conversation with Lukas."

There's a silence, as if to commemorate their fallen comrade, missing presumed dead – as dead as one whose brain activity ceases to register on the Nooby machine quantum signature detector.

"OK, when he was trying to persuade the bad guys there were options, in the last seconds before he, before they did whatever they did... He asked what if *they* could live a lot longer. Well, we know that's possible. We know we have it almost sorted. So what if we put that on the front burner, and, as soon as it's ready, *announce it to the public as free for anyone who can make it work?*"

Jen nods. "Imagine a world where everyone can live a thousand years plus. That would focus everyone sharply on running out of resources."

Nooby grimaces. "And what about exponential population growth?"

"What of it?"   Jimmy looks serenely unconcerned. "Why would anyone want a huge family instantly, relatively speaking, when they have a thousand years ahead of them? And anyway, all that does is push forward the date when we have to deal with the resource crunches we would have anyway if people carry on thinking short-term."

That night, Jimmy feels the familiar sensation in his head.

What's new?

Jimmy summarises recent events.

Wow. I'm sorry about Lukas. He turned out to be quite a find. Wish I'd known him, I mean so as not to forget him. Great progress though. What's next?

We're planning on putting age-deferral on the front burner, then going public.

Interesting idea. What will you do when the planet fills up?

What did you do when its carrying capacity dramatically reduced when the climate went to hell?

Not pretty. Dog eat dog. Civil wars.

But this would be different. Time to plan, people with a long view.

**And a smart team driving events behind the scenes. I
have my doubts but it's your timeline.**

Thanks for acknowledging that.

Any regrets?

You mean the past, Mel and all that?

Yes, but also other things.

*Losing Lukas is a biggie. The chicken pox thing was
avoidable. We shouldn't have put the technology on display,
lucky we got away with misdirection the way we did. The rest:
Mel, Diane, can't go back and change things.*

**No. But let me check in with you every now and then. I
may still have ideas for you.**

Thanks. The presence has gone. What was that about
regrets, and you can't go back and change things? Who was
it again who had actually tried to do that?

But back to here and now: Steve and Maddy are getting
frail, and Jimmy decides to let them in on the story. He takes
a trip to Palo Alto, and drives his rental car to the familiar
old house. Maddy walks him to the living room, where Steve
apologizes for not getting up. "Son, I'm sorry, the old bones
aren't what they used to be."

"That's just it, dad. There's this project I've been working
on for years, that's been seriously held up since I lost Dianne."
He explains without bringing in his future self. "We are still
a way off releasing this to the general public, but I think
we can reverse some of the worst effects of ageing already.
And I want you guys to have that option, though it is strictly
speaking illegal without proper trials."

Maddy looks serious, weighing things up. "Son, what
happens when the whole world can live for – how long did

you say?"

"Mom, I'm not sure how long. We can't know until we've pushed it to the limit. I don't see why we can't extend it to centuries. We can control programmed cell death, and that includes stopping cancer, the less desirable side of allowing cells to divide indefinitely. We can reprogram cells that have deviated from design. It's not just one thing, it's a bag of tricks that comes from understanding in detail how everything works. The marketing spin is *live for a thousand years*, though the fine print says 'not guaranteed, terms and conditions apply'."

"But what about over-population? Water shortages and so on?" Maddy looks at Steve for support. He nods grimly.

Jimmy repeats the pitch: "Longer life means those things happen sooner but we are more likely to worry if the problem happens in our own lifetime – not talking for people like us who care already, but the general population. Think about climate change. Would the fat cats be so casual about letting it all slide away if the worst was going to happen in their lifetime? This way we get rid of the mentality of stealing from the future, because it's our future too."

"Maddy and I need to think about this son. You aren't a crazy person. I know this because I've seen you close up for so many years. But this is not something we had to think about before."

Five years on, the longevity technology is testing well enough to go public. Climate change denial is a spent force but change is still too slow. So the plan is on. Jimmy invites the media to his private island, all pretence of low-key inconspicuous operation dropped. There's an obvious message to get out, Dianne's rejuvenated parents. They willingly take part, no argument there. But there's another less obvious message to get out. He summons Esmerelda to his den.

"Esmerelda, do you remember what you were wearing when you were abducted?"

"I think so. But I don't have those clothes any more."

"Can you find something that looks pretty much the same, and make yourself look pretty much as you did then?"

"I'm not sure if I can look as miserable."

"No need. In fact, the opposite. We just need certain people who used you to get a message when we go live on worldwide TV. Whatever they did to Lukas, we aren't beaten."

A large media contingent assembles. There are wild rumours flying around about this mysterious latter-day Howard Hughes, a wealthy recluse with his own Greek island, who prefers to keep his life and details of his fortune private. And who now, totally out of character, is inviting the world's media to his parlour. Jimmy appears at the podium with Jen and Nooby. Esmerelda is in the background, looking confident and self-assured, positioned so the cameras have to catch her unless they are tightly focused on Jimmy. Next to her are two fit young people, who look to be in their mid-twenties.

Jimmy stares straight down the lens of the nearest video camera. "People of the world: I have a great gift for all of you, the gift of life. For the last twenty years, I have been working on the causes of ageing, and I believe it is now possible for any person who does not suffer a catastrophic accident to live at least a thousand years. Right now the technology is expensive but with a few more years of work, everyone will be able to afford it. So that it can happen sooner, I am releasing all I know for anyone to research free of charge, no patents, no royalties.

"For such long life to make sense, we all need to live as if the planet will still be a viable home for humanity in a thousand years, and moderate our use of resources to suit. We will have to make a shift from having large families early in life to small families late in life. Many things will have to change, but I believe most of that change will be for the better.

"I would like to introduce the parents of my first wife. I lost her tragically in a plane crash. We can't fix that sort of problem yet. But her parents, and I'm proud to call them mom and dad, are both over 90 years old, and were frail and barely able to walk 5 years ago.

"Mom, dad, walk out front to meet the press." He gestures to them. *If Esmerelda wasn't on camera before, she will be now.*

Maddy and Steve stride out confidently into popping flashes, leaving Esmerelda behind, their skin smooth and unwrinkled, their hair back to its original colour, no hint of grey.

Steve stands next to Jimmy, and says, "When they applied the procedure to us, we were willing to be guinea pigs because we didn't have long to live. We now play tennis, something we had to give up more than 10 years ago, and don't have those embarrassing senior moments we used to have all too often."

Flashes go off like crazy, and Jimmy thanks Steve, who walks back to Esmerelda with Maddy. Esmerelda steps forward and gives them each a hug as soon as the media focus is back on Jimmy, her job done.

"So what changes will there be for the better, besides living longer and not losing those you love prematurely? We can no longer take the attitude that the future doesn't matter because it's a future generation's problem. We will have a new motivation to cease practices such as polluting as if we are the last generation on the planet, and the next century is beyond our horizon. We will have to find alternatives to non-renewable energy sources, and we will have to stop climate change. Or wear the consequences ourselves, rather than stealing our children's and grandchildren's future.

"Any questions?"

32 Phone call

THE RAIN pelts down. It rains in summer in Johannesburg, but not usually this much. He picks up the phone, dials the number, more in trepidation than expectation. On the third ring, it picks up. Answering machine.

"When you said, 'see you on the weekend', I kind of expected to find you before the weekend. It's Saturday, 10 am, and I would like to hear from you."

He drops the phone, sags to the floor, no chair handy. Jimmy Anderson, the smartest guy in class, the stupidest guy around girls.

How many times has this happened?

Glossary

Afrikaans pronunciation notes

a a single "a" is pronounced like an English "uh"; "**aa**" is a longer version of an English "ah"

aai like an English "i" as in "like"

ei like an English "ay" as in "hay"

g like a Scottish "ch"

i short version of English "i" as in "hiss"

ie like an English word-ending "y" or "ie" as in "indie"

j like an English "y" as in "year"

oe shorter version of English "oo"

u like an English "i" as in "is"

v like an English "f"

w like an English "v"

Potentially unfamiliar terms

Afrikaans Dutch-derived language of the ruling white minority (Afrikaners) in the *apartheid* era.

aka also known as.

ANC African National Congress, banned with leadership in exile at the start of our narrative and the ruling party of South Africa from 1994.

apartheid Afrikaans: separateness. Legally-enforced segregation and racially-based politics in South Africa 1948-1994.

Auckland Park slightly more conservative neighbour of *Melville*.

blerrie mild Afrikaans curse: bloody.

Boer colonial-era name for Afrikaners (hence Boer War, or Anglo-Boer War); in modern Afrikaans: farmer.

Botha, PW last prime minister and first executive president of South Africa; hardline militarist succeed by last apartheid president, FW *de Klerk*.

braai Afrikaans: barbecue; also South African English for barbecue.

broeder Afrikaans: brother; shorthand for *Afrikaner Broederbond* (Afrikaner Brotherhood) member, a secret society that formed an old boys' network to counter economic and political dominance of English-speaking South Africans.

Cape Town South Africa's oldest city and legislative capital, where parliament sits.

crunchie a rolled-oats biscuit popular in South Africa, usually cooked in a shallow rectangular pan then cut into squares; similar to Anzac biscuits in Australia, though the latter are usually round.

de Klerk, FW last apartheid president: freed Mandela with whom he was jointly awarded a Nobel Peace Prize.

Democratic Party (DP) liberal opposition to the *Nats* and later *ANC*; became the Democratic Alliance (DA) in 2000 during a brief dalliance with the "New" *National Party*.

donder Afrikaans: thunder.   Often used as a mild curse in conjunction with a stronger one for emphasis; also means "beat up".

elastoplast generic term for sticky plaster (a common brand in South Africa).

FORTRAN programming language used for mainly numerical computation, as in physics.

generaal Afrikaans: general.

GRE graduate record examination: a standardised test used mainly for entry to US graduate schools.

group areas the *apartheid* Group Areas Act divided urban areas into zones for racial groups and Blacks who owned homes or businesses in the "wrong" areas were generally forced to sell on a willing buyer unwilling seller basis, or give them up to the government for scant compensation.

ja Afrikaans: yes.

jislaaik Afrikaans: expression of surprise.

Johannesburg South Africa's biggest, wealthiest city, aka Joburg.

kak Afrikaans: crap.

klap Afrikaans: slap.

koeksister sweet confection of dough plaited, deep fried and plunged into syrup. May include a hint of ginger.

kommandant Afrikaans: commandant; lieutenant colonel-equivalent in the apartheid army.

koppie Afrikaans: low hill.

korporaal Afrikaans: corporal.

lifie surf lifesaver: lifeguard in American.

M masters degree (common usage among Afrikaans speakers).

melktert Afrikaans: a milky baked custard tart (sweet not savoury but not unsavoury) flavoured with cinnamon.

Melville trendy suburb of *Johannesburg*.

MK see *Umkhonto we Sizwe*.

Natal province in pre-apartheid South Africa; now kwaZulu-Natal.

National Party aka *Nats*: the ruling party of apartheid, 1948-1994. Became the New National Party in 1997 but fooled no one and merged with the ANC in 2005 after increasingly poor election results.

oke Afrikaans slang: roughly translates as "bloke".

PF permanent force members – often a derogatory label used by conscripts in the apartheid military.

Pretoria South Africa's administrative capital: headquarters of the civil service.

RF radio frequency – generic term for communications using radio.

Schrödinger's cat a thought experiment used by physicist Erwin Schrödinger to illustrate potential absurdities arising from interpretations of quantum theory, in which a cat can simultaneously be alive and dead until observed by an outsider.

sersant Afrikaans: sergeant.

Silicon Graphics aka SGI: maker of fast computers initially only for graphics but later for large-scale computation.

South Coast coastal *Natal* holiday region south of Durban; includes Margate and Shelly Beach.

trommel Afrikaans: trunk.

Tukkies University of Pretoria: nickname based on its original identity as the Pretoria branch of Transvaal University College (TUC).

Umkhonto we Sizwe Spear of the Nation (in several African languages): ANC's military wing, aka *MK*.

UNIX computer operating system popular in academia, forerunner of free systems like Linux.

vok Afrikaans curse; hence *vokken* and *vokkal*.

white noise random sound with an even spread over the spectrum: similar to static of an untuned radio.

windgat Afrikaans: windy orifice.

Wits University of the Witwatersrand (last word usually pronounced the Afrikaans way); sometimes pronounced with no hint of irony as if "Wits" is an English word. Conservative but with some history of opposing apartheid.

Woolworths in South Africa a food and clothing chain with a quality image (unrelated to the UK and Australian Woolworths; named after the US Woolworth with an added "s", taking advantage of a loophole in trade mark laws; most closely related to UK retail chain Marks & Spencer); aka *Woolies*.

Acknowledgments

I would like to thank Ed de la Rey, Jane Nash and my wife Fiona Semple for proof reading, and Anthea Hide and Nhlanhla Mabaso for finding some residual typos.

Also by this author

Fiction

No Tomorrow, 2nd edition, RAMpage Research, 2007, ISBN 978-0-9804510-0-9

Nonfiction

An Object-Oriented Library for Shared-Memory Parallel Simulations, 2nd edition, RAMpage Research, 2008, ISBN 978-0-9804510-2-3

Printed in Great Britain
by Amazon